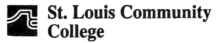

SECRETS

SECRETS

▼▼▼

KELVIN CHRISTOPHER JAMES

VILLARD BOOKS
NEW YORK
1993

A portion of this work was originally published in *BOMB* magazine.

Library of Congress Cataloging-in-Publication Data

James, Kelvin Christopher.
Secrets / by Kelvin Christopher James.
p.   cm.
ISBN 0-679-42409-1
I. Title.
PS3560.A386S4   1993
813'.54—dc20   93-12690

Manufactured in the United States of America

9   8   7   6   5   4   3   2

First Edition

Book design by Debbie Glasserman

To our children,
with confidence.

Smackers of appreciation to Joy-o-Joy, oodles of thank-yous upon Dougie-Doug, and especially lovely gold stars for Jackie and Jeanne and Maureen and Diane and Amy for levering the wagon along, and, certainly, even better than that for my loyal posse.

SECRETS

▼▼▼

THE RAID ON Dosaro's was risky, daring discovery, though, for Uxann, well worth the spoils. Those plump, perfectly ripened guanabanas, their soursop scent pulling butterflies seeking nectar. For her, the prize was the taste of them. The wet of her tongue to the fruit's creamy meat, a mix dissolving aroma into memory, a spark giving back food its life. This was the delight she craved, which just thinking of surged a gush in her mouth.

For a half-mile stretch along the road to school, the fruit orchard tempted from behind a six-feet-high stave and wire barricade. There was a watchman—the mingy owner, who, anytime he caught a vaps to, patroled the orchard himself. A mean, close man who stalked tiptoe with bull-pistle in hand, and had caught and whipped a few. A wicked man who'd sometimes bear a hair-trigger shotgun that itched for a notch. But nothing he did could fence the scents on the air, and several students were canny enough to get in and out with whatever. That chubby Uxann was champ at this was her secret.

Walking the route five days a week, she had swallowed her spit while watching and waiting. Then, dawdling home one afternoon, she saw what she thought was a stave askew. Five further schooldays, because of weather or company going home, she waited to check. And it was so. With a pull and a shift, she had a way in. She told her best friend and cousin, Keah.

Now, Uxann stood on the grassy edge of the dirt road, her arms crossed tightly over her broad chest, feeling stubborn and stupid about it. But determined not to give in, she watched Keah return through the tall grass that bordered Dosaro's grove.

Keah lightly jumped the two-foot flood drain, disturbing a swirl of buzzing things. As she scrambled up to the roadway, the insects re-settled and disappeared in the stagnant mess. Keah dusted her hands on her skirt, clinking the glinting silver bracelets over her wrists. "God! What a relief!" she exclaimed. "Been holding that in since recess."

Despite herself, Uxann asked, "So what prevent you recess-time?"

Keah giggled smugly. "You know," she said.

Uxann did know. Preddy. These days it was with him Keah used up all her recess, squeezing together into whatever half-private corner they could find on the schoolgrounds. Last month she was same way with Raimau. Last term it was Sharry.

Keah said, "Anyhow, we figured that maybe it'd be better if you watchman, and we go pick. You have cleaner ears, and so on, yu'know . . ."

Uxann listened grimly.

". . . then afterwards, we share up equal-equal."

Uxann kept her eyes straight on Keah's face, and remained silent.

Sucking her teeth, Keah said, "So why you so vex already? I ent even finish yet."

"I not vex. I just waiting," said Uxann. She jerked her fierce stare away, unable to stand the smugness behind Keah's thin, earnest face. Her soft, rich cocoa-brown prettyface smooth-talking like butter wouldn't melt in the mouth, with her deceitfulness sparking the smiling eyes.

"Uxann," she coaxed, "we must have a watchman. Suppose Dosaro come by and catch we, eh? We have to have a watchman. And you true-true sharper-eyed than me. You know that. And whatever me and Preddy get, we go share with you." As she finished, she cast quick eyes to the curve down the road from which Preddy would show.

Uxann gritted her teeth harder, and glared away in rage. So now she had clean ears, huh? And nothing between them, too, they must think. So she had to watchman because she could see and hear sharp. Didn't they think her brain was sharp, too? At least sharp enough to figure out why they wanted her standing like a statue by the roadside, while Keah and Preddy Dassen went alone in old Dosaro's orange grove.

Steady-eyed, curtaining off her intuitions, she asked, "Who is this 'we'? And what it is you and Preddy want me watchman? How come he here at all? This was we plan. Alone. Nobody help me find this guanabana tree, or this hole in, yu'know."

Keah's eyes fell. "Uxann, don't make it so hard, nuh." Then, eyes darting up, defiant and spiting, she went on, "And why you have to bring up Preddy for everything so, huh? You jealous, or what?"

It was this swift contempt that cowed Uxann, that herded her to escape into indifference, behind a face placid as butter. "No! I don't care," she said. "I'll watch if you want."

"Well, okay, then, that'd be for the best. And you know I wouldn't try to fool you." Then she walked off to the bend in the road where Preddy would appear, bracelets jangling as she tossed back a strayed left braid.

Uxann remained where she was, face unrevealing. Yet in the dark quiet of her mind, her outrage barred compliance. It was open knowledge that the next due traffic was the Valpariso bus at five o'clock. There was nothing to watch, and they knew it. Knew that she did, too. Yet they were so careless at slighting her. So bold, it cramped her throat and made her shudder. She would get Keah back for this, she swore. Even as her hurt sprung in her eyes and she whimpered to herself, "They never ever want me around. . . ."

She looked at Keah, waiting fifteen yards away—tense, the sunlight catching the glaze of sweat at her neck. All of a sudden, the sight of her was sour, and Uxann wanted to be away. To leave them to their business and raid Dosaro's another time—by herself.

But to deceive them better, she decided to wait until Preddy came and they'd stolen into the fruit grove, believing they had her playing watchdog to their rendezvous.

▼▼▼

As SOON AS they'd gone through the hole in the fence, Uxann walked off for home. To kill the extra time she had, she decided on a track through the woods. She knew where there was a bird setting on a clutch of two speckled brown eggs. Several times already she had climbed the low tree and inspected the nest. She'd never seen the mother, but, always aware of the anxiety spying from nearby, she was careful as she snuggled the warm globes to her eyelids and cheeks. But although handling the eggs gave a thrill, Uxann yearned to discover and observe the distressed mother. Her chance might be this time, a thought pulling her swiftly through the murmuring forest.

Freed from the sense of eyes on her, Uxann relaxed into herself. Her short-stepped mincing gave way to a loose stride, balanced on the balls of her feet, light on the leafy forest track. And because not always sight gave secrets, she kept her passage nearly soundless, and listened to the forest be alive. Heard its breathy leaves whisper. Heard private talk in whistles and tweets and chirps and squawks of tensions and territories, and rituals and harmonies.

With each stride, her book bag, slung across her right shoulder, beat on her left hip solidly, in rhythm with her breathing, her heartbeat, the vital pulse of the forest. Just her movement, her rustling through the great, quiet place, comforted. Here in the forest she felt at home, native like a wild thing. Here her plumpness fitted. When she jumped, there was no threatening thump—the natural trace had spring enough to absorb her solid presence. She didn't have to think light, or prim and tight. She could move bold here, could prance and spring, undam the cramp she lived under others' eyes. Let go to how she was—big and floppy, muscled slack and jouncy. She hummed the chorus of the popular caiso, pausing to dance a dip step natural to the melody. She didn't feel clumsy at all, but lighthearted close to gladness that she was big, and she could move so well.

At the stream beyond which the nest waited, she paused to catch her breath. Stealth was important here. She rested against a large boulder and scouted the stones across the shallows. Satisfied with a path, she hop-skipped to the broadest raised one and squatted down, cupping a handful of the gurgling water to her face, lip-sipping, before letting most splash back to the brisk stream. Again and again she repeated the soothing cooling, until gradually a complete peacefulness took her, and ceased the background rustle of breezed leaves, and stilled the chaos of birdcalling, and the whole world paused as if an angel floated by. With Uxann caught poised, hands reaching forward to the water, worship shivering through her.

After the while she was released and, blinking about, slowly returned to the forest and its sounds. Contented and drained, she decided against bothering the bird, and turned to retrace her steps to the track for home.

The distance shrunk in her daze of thoughts, with some surprise Uxann found herself at the end of her shortcut and out of the woods. A hundred yards more, through an abandoned pasture, and she was at the vegetable garden she and Paps cultivated back of their house. She wandered through the neat beds, straightening the tomatoes' supports here, moulding a lettuce or cauliflower there. A tiny spot of yellow caught her eye among the sprouting corn. It was a bursting zinnia pod; almost no plant at all, but a green bud giving way to the push of the gold petals underneath. A bold blossom competing with the sunlight. Sprung up out of place, though. Uxann bent close to pull the fresh speck.

A loud cackling erupted from the backyard. A hen, either alarmed or exclaiming she had laid an egg. Uxann straightened up and started for the ruckus. Noisy fowl is quiet dinnertime, she heard Paps repeat in her head, and thought of Mr. Mongoose, close in the bush out there, patiently listening to his dinner bell. She followed the excited clucking to a skinny, speckled brown hen, and found in a banana stool the nest with three eggs in it, one warm.

"Oh-ho!" she murmured to herself. "An evening layer." And with a smile at thwarting Mr. Mongoose's mealtime, she hitched up her skirt to a pouch and took them all.

Returned to the backyard garden, a copse of laden pigeon peas set her thinking dinner and, planning as she went along, Uxann decided to cook Paps an extra fa-

vorite this evening. She plucked some knobby, fat pur-
pling pods. Seyeh loved them boiled down in coconut
milk. And there was still a piece of smoked manicou
from his last upriver hunt. Yes, stew it all up and give
Seyeh a treat, she would. Since he certainly loved her
stir of the pots. Content with her plans, Uxann headed
for the outside kitchen back of the house.

She put the food in a washpan and set to lighting the
fires—in the coalpot, a slow one for the manicou stew,
and in the fireside, a searing hardwood flame. While the
fires caught, she went to change into home clothes. But
one step in the house she stopped short, hearing the
hoarse, hearty, whispered banter, the coupled laughter.
End-of-fortnight sounds. Payday, and Paps home and
drunk early with female company. With all the afternoon's excitements it had slipped her mind. She could
forget about him being any part of her cooking plans
tonight.

Uxann bit her bottom lip hard to contain her disappointment, but couldn't restrain the sudden wet rush at
her eyes. So, sniffles and blinks, she turned to her room,
swallowing the choke that heated her neck.

By sunset the meal was done and she had eaten a
solitary dinner. After washing up, she went down the
backyard to check the animals. A pass by the sty
showed the pigs rooting and snorting around as usual.
From farther down the yard came the occasional goat-

bleat as they settled down in their regular spot under the calabash tree. Most of the fowl had found comfortable crooks among the cocoa-tree branches. A squawking leghorn pullet and a clean-necked cockerel were flying up seeking late accommodation. And, as was their habit at end of day, the two zebus—her destination—stood outside their stall after wandering home.

Uxann liked caring for the big, hump-backed cows, Boobee and Zug. Despite their size and strength, their always drooling mouths and timid eyes gave them a shy, helpless look. And the smell of them, too—solid, funky, of sweat and grass and corn. Uxann heaped the nightly rations into their feed buckets, and filled the water trough. On her way back to the house, the evening showers began.

Waking, Uxann sat up quickly, staring at the liquid beam streaming into her room through the window, the beautiful moonlight a surprise as she recalled the roar of rain that had soothed her to sleep. A low, sad bawl rose in the night—a zebu's moan, muffled, miserable—and

Uxann realized it was not the moonlight had awoken her.

She knew the problem. The stupid zebu, frightened by the lightning, had blundered out of the yardpen. It had probably taken all of that storm, her moan sounded wet and long-suffering enough. Uxann half-listened for sounds of Paps moving to the situation, but, with last evening in mind, she didn't expect him. The zebu moaned again. Uxann sighed and got out of bed.

Skirts of her nightdress gathered up and knotted to pantaloons, her feet in Paps' tall-top rubber boots, Uxann opened the kitchen door to the brilliant moonlight. It was after midnight, the scorpion's tail high in the sky. A light, cool breeze rippled through the trees, making the fresh-washed leaves sparkle. The night smelled clean, crisp, sweet. She shuffled out in the big boots to find the poor lost beast.

The cow had not blundered. She had stolen out and plundered the feedhouse, and couldn't return to the yardpen because the gate had swung shut. Probably seeking shelter, the greedy brute had jammed herself under the brief overhang of the feedhouse roof. There Uxann found her—it was Boobee—with corn grains sticking among her dribbly guilty whiskers, and trembling so badly that her shivers made the wooden shack rattle. There was nothing to prevent her from moving.

Still the zebu just stood there, squeezing against the shed, looming cold and sheepish.

Uxann couldn't stay vexed at the sorry sight. Hands flat against the zebu's bulging belly and rump, she pushed hard, leaning into it, more stubborn than the cow, until the beast budged and started off walking stiffly, swinging her head, reluctant as a sad man to the gallows.

Back in the stall, the cow was still cold, shivering pale steam into the moonlight. Uxann searched the dim corners for something to warm her. A lump of loosely folded cloth, suggesting cozy homes for scratchy crawlers like scorpions and centipedes, turned out to be an old canvas hammock. Gritting teeth against the danger of poisonous stings, she carefully picked it up and shook it briefly, then tossed it over Boobee's trembling back.

It fell unevenly, so she went around the other side to make adjustments. Reaching up to pull the cover, her body jammed against Boobee's shivering belly. A rude, heady steam from the tremors filled her nose. It was warm, almost hot, carrying a pungent smell that gave her pause from a thrill, made her mouth spring. And without thinking, she pressed her face into the zebu's moist hide, burrowing her nose and mouth through the coarse pelt until she could smell its damp spicy taint and taste the salty steam.

Some sound from the yard's night, and Uxann was anxiously searching. But the bland moonlight remained empty of betrayal. She went back around to the other side of the cow, where she was concealed by its bulk. And there, heart beating fast, she stooped to pursue her craving. Bending under Boobee's belly to the udders, she sucked a long, swollen teat into her mouth.

Grunting low and contented, the cow shifted her hind legs slightly, accommodating Uxann as she rolled the turgid teat in her mouth, suckling and pulling until, past an initial bitterness, there burst a vital spurt. A sweet warm stream she slavered at, and slurped and barely paused to lick her lips. The milk, her guilt, the rain-cleaned moonlight, the quivering beast above her—all of the moment gaining a flavour more savoury. Like salt to good pepper, it made the hot spicy.

▼▼▼

EVEN BEFORE SHE got to the backyard fence on her way home from school, Uxann heard the dogs. From the garden she saw them tied up under the bread-fruit tree, barking and yelping with too much enthusiasm for any creature wearing chains. A gruff echo after was their masters' voices from the front yard. As she headed for her room, she yelled, "Ah home, Paps."

Changed into her house clothes, she found him in the kitchen. With a big grin, he said, "Sharpen yuh teeth, Girl Chile, an' loosen yuh appetite. Is quail tomorrow." His eyes sparked excitement.

Uxann clapped delightedly. "In truth, Paps? In truth? Oh, goodness," she cried, rushing to him and clasping his arm close. Paps stiffened slightly, and she let go in a moment; however happy the time, he wasn't a one much for hugging. So, to help contain her pleasure, she drew a cup of rainwater from the earthen pitcher by the sink, and drank it down slowly.

Paps was reaching up tippy-toes to the upper shelves, his hands exploring. "Yuh remember where ah put de shells, de buckshot?"

"Uh-huh, Paps. Is me who put dem away, and is not up dere." She had safed the shells in a tight-covered one-pound biscuit can. She took the can from under the sink and handed it to him.

"Girl, ah don't know what ah'd do without you," he said.

"You'd manage, Paps," she said, although that didn't represent her gratified happiness.

He went to his room for the gun, and was soon lead-ing the hunting party out of the front yard. "Girl Chile, wish me luck, or we eating breadfruit tomorrow," he called.

"Good luck, Paps," she called back. "Aim before you fire." And smiled smugly at hearing the banter and laughter she had roused.

▼▼▼

By half past five she was done with eating and home-work and washing up and everything. And the house was getting close around her. Especially since, off and on with the breeze, she could hear the activity down by the roadside standpipe: yells, clangs of empty buckets careless to the ground, boisterous laughter. Sounds tot-ing water for the night. Cries of young folks' fun. Noise she wanted part of. Except that with her in-house run-ning water, she had no reason. And although Paps hadn't actually banned her, he didn't like her there. Was infradig, he said.

But Paps was gone hunting, having his good time. And the house was so quiet, and close, and lonely. And if he asked, she could always create a reason: needed to clear up a school question; decided to stretch her legs;

heard voices in her head. So, armed with mad plan, she broke out.

At first, because of the gloaming, she couldn't make out who was who. It was many, though—girls grouped near the standpipe itself, and boys clumped in twos and threes across the road. As she got close and was recognized, there was a little hush and whispering. Some surprised one burst out, "Look who's coming."

By then she'd made out Eralee and Keah, and made for them hopefully. And it was all right. Eralee came towards her with smile and frown. "What you doing here, girl?" she asked, so bold, so open, Uxann at once felt welcome.

"Allyou so scandalous out here, I sneak out to see," she said.

"And yuh father gone hunting so you could." This from Roonee, who, arms akimbo, was snaking her head, eyeing like a Miss Know-it-all.

Uxann smiled sheepishly and shrugged.

"She father gone too," provided Keah. "Dat's why she know, and dat's why she here so long." A private olive-branch offer; and Uxann met Keah's eyes without a clash.

"Dat's not why ah here," Roonee said with a giggle. "Dat's how ah here."

Someone suggested, "Why you here is across de road with eyes falling out he head for you."

This brought on a burst of knowing giggles, everyone

suddenly searching through the boys clustered across the road, and sharing their discoveries in whispers.

On their side, the dusk-hid boys, eyes white in shadow faces, were finding courage and trying tactics. One fellow was earnestly persuading another—a smaller boy, a brother, maybe. After a while, the little boy drifted over and approached a girl. Among the others, a space of quiet opened for him as he went to his target and whispered into her ear. Not a word; just a proud toss of head, a look of disdain. That was all her reply. The little fellow, though, skipped back across the road as if happily rewarded.

None of these boys—Seyeh's future workers— would bother her, the overseer's daughter, Uxann convinced herself. So, from a face of placid nonchalance, she watched the boldness build. Keeping her largeness unobtrusive, she could feel excitement passing around like a mist, could almost absorb the intrigue through her skin. By now, in the deep dark under the roadside trees fifteen feet off, a body—or bodies—might disappear. On both sides the groups must've realized this, for now the messaging back and forth became more personal. In the group Uxann made a foursome, a tall bony boy, softly in honey tones, was asking Eralee to walk privately with him: down by the river, through the woods after school. With lower-eyed looks and simpering smiles, she promised only maybes.

Eventually, as the numbers dwindled, the questing died and Uxann reluctantly said her good-byes. She slunk away, quick into the gloom, awkward with the fact that no boy had looked her way. Near the turn into her front gate, just at vision's limit, a pleading grunt and a snicker, then a bulkiness in the semidark detached abruptly, a couple parting to opposite paths. Uxann stopped quietly and kept her distance until they were well gone. They brought to mind that she had not seen Keah leave, or with whom, so glazed-eyed she had been at hiding herself.

Still, leaving the scene, having been some part of it, was almost a relief. She was somewhat like the rest headed home, some disappointed, others wistful, a few with priceless rewards. For it was whispered that, out of others' minding, some rendezvous were made and met. Although she'd never speak on it, one Uxann knew of from the horse's mouth. As best friends, Keah had sometimes confided.

▼▼▼

FRIDAY A WEEK later, a saint day, school let out at afternoon recess. Because of their sometimishness, Uxann usually walked home alone, keeping deliberate distance ahead or behind the others going her way. Today, intending to cut off and make trace to the fruit trees, she chose behind. Once on the road, though, Eralee dawdled back from her usual threesome until Uxann had to walk with her.

Soon she was spreading the news: "Yuh hear what happen with Keah?"

Uxann had missed Keah at school the last few days, but figured it to her own general aloofness and Keah busy at romances. "No," she said, "what?"

"Well, yu'know she not coming back."

"Not coming back?" Uxann echoed. "Yuh mean to school?"

"What else I could mean?" said Eralee with coy impatience.

"Why? What happen to she?"

"You know. Yu'just pretending yu'don't know," teased Eralee.

"No, I really don't. I was studying for mih exams. So I was too busy to know anything," Uxann excused lamely.

A few quiet paces along, Eralee relented. "Well, de nuns expel she."

"Expel she? Keah?" Uxann echoed, astonished at the news. "What she do?"

Eralee skipped a few extra-long steps, picked up a stone and threw it without hope at a scurrying grounddove, then returned to Uxann's side and regarded her smugly. "Well, Sister Moran ketch she and Preddy behind de tool shed in de vegetable garden doing nasty," she said triumphantly.

Uxann closed her hanging jaw. There was a word, the rude, real word she knew, but was unable to bring to her mouth. She said instead, "Yu'mean . . . bulling?"

Eralee shrugged. "If yuh want. Yeah, like cow in heat in de bull pen."

Uxann flushed as she recalled the recent scene at Dosaro's arbour: Keah waiting ready for Preddy. Yes, the passion of Keah's protests and pleas then fitted this. But how could they have gone crazy enough to try it on school grounds? "And what dey do to Preddy?" she asked.

"Oh, he expel, too. But he say he was leaving school anyhow. He say yuh father line up a job for him brush-cutting under de cocoa. He was only waiting for rainy season, he say."

Letting the reference to her father's overseer status pass, Uxann asked, "So, what Keah doing?"

"She home. Everybody know about it. She shame to go out de house."

"Oh, God," Uxann exclaimed, "better she than me."

They chatted the matter all the long graveled road to the village, Uxann bypassing her shortcut intentions for the thrill of this spicy gossip; she could raid Dosaro's over the weekend. At the junction to her house, grateful to generosity, she promised Eralee, "Monday morning I'll have some mandarin orange and a few sapodilla for you, okay."

The two others, waiting for Eralee, looked back inviting a good-bye wave. And when Uxann did, they returned it with smiles. It was a happy moment for Uxann: She felt in, in the know of the gossip, one of the group. Thoughts abuzz over it all, she went home.

▼▼▼

ALTHOUGH IT WAS too early in the season, rains came in such torrents that the river bridge was flooded and school had to be closed for three days. With the constant downpouring outside, Uxann spent most of the time reading ahead for her schoolwork, especially in geography and arithmetic. In these subjects she had grown accustomed to compliments from the sisters. Since Paps went to work as usual, the house was hers during the day. When not studying, she cooked in the inside kitchen, scooting into the showers for this or that herb or vegetable from the garden. Each day Paps returned home to extra-tantalizing aromas of dishes meant to excite and please.

Thursday afternoon the sun came out, the clouds white and high, the skies clean blue. No school, though. The river was still up, the bridge closed. The house was a hollow of quiet, a hushed cave from which Uxann listened to the hum of nature being busy, the flit and twitter, the rustle and rush that pulsed the vibrant scene. At the window in the front room, she sat peeking from behind barely flapped curtains.

Two toddlers from the neighbour's had ventured into her front yard to play in a mound of leftover plastering soft sand. Three, four years old, and naked but for snot and dribble, they were delighting in throwing sand at each other. Rushing and stumbling at it. Falling, scrambling about, raiding one another's ammunition piles. Uxann smiled, feeling their pleasure, not long ago her own indulgence, shivering with memory of the solid fall of fine river sand trickling over her, the surprise of cool without wet.

Notwithstanding the hilarity, it was only time before the babies' eyes would suffer the fine fun sand. Yet Uxann hesitated at going out to stop their play. They might see her intrusion as chasing them, and she dreaded that impression. So, at edge of the chair, she peeped and worried, wistful at the toddlers' carefree antics.

The cool sharp touch on her neck came with a throaty raspy whisper: "Jumbie!" Uxann's mind emptied. Terrified, she scrambled from the chair and into the near corner, crouching and gasping in air to power a scream, searching back wildly for the threat. But immediately, the fright in her lungs exploded as a bark of relieved laughter. For it was only Keah standing there, caught in her stealthy stance, her face silly between triumph and scare at Uxann's overreaction.

Then laughter took over, collapsing them completely. Keah hugged her belly, stooping over, stomping around the room wheezing as if merriment were choking her to silence. Uxann, weak on the floor, was slapping the smooth morah boards until her palms stung, trying to hurt the mirth away and save herself from the reckless glee. It took its own teasing time, going away moments to minutes before re-erupting in unexpected fits.

"I didn't hear you at all," Uxann quavered at last.

"De top of de kitchen side door was open, so ah just reach over and unlatch it and come in. It so quiet, ah didn't think you was home. Then ah see you peeping by de window, so ah decide to fool you. . . ."

The fright scene turned funny recalled, they had to exhaust this new burst of laughter before a teary-eyed Uxann agreed, "Well, girl, you suck seed and I suck salt, 'cause I was frighten in truth."

Keah snapped her fingers as if suddenly remembering. "Oh, God, Uxann," she exclaimed, "I laugh so much, I have to pee. Where's dis inside WC dey say allyuh have?"

Uxann proudly led her to the toilet.

▼▼▼

TRY AS SHE might, Uxann couldn't put her mouth to bring up the expulsion business. They skirted it with why she was looking at—not spying on—the children outside. They marveled at the storming weather. Then, the house new to Keah, Uxann walked her through, stopping in her own room. Keah checked the view from her window, and admired her starter pot of herb seedlings. All the time, like talking around a third person, they avoided Keah's trouble.

Then a safe topic occurred to Keah. "Yuh know why I here, though?"

"No," said Uxann.

"Yuh mean Seyeh ent tell you?"

"No," Uxann said again.

"Well, I here to work for allyuh."

"Work?"

"Yeah."

"Work doing what?" said Uxann, the idea striking her as funny.

"I don't know." Keah grinned. "Is Pa arrange it with Seyeh." She rolled her eyes as if it were all beyond her.

Amusement ready to bubble up, Uxann asked mockofficiously, "And what job you looking for, young lady?"

Which removed all seriousness from the puzzle, and had them soon laughing themselves silly.

▼▼▼

WHEN PAPS CAME home, he sat them down around the dining-room table. Straight to the point, he said, "Keah going to work for we. . . ."

As if rehearsed, Uxann and Keah interrupted with suppressed titters.

Seyeh looked at them, puzzled, then continued, "She go start Monday. She will come over in de afternoon, do a little housework, wash a few clothes, and leave after dinner. If she want to, she will eat dinner with we."

Again the girls giggled in mysterious unison.

Seyeh said, "Ah glad to see allyuh getting along so smooth. Dat's how ah want it to be." He addressed Keah: "You could stay a little while if you

want, but dey expecting you back home by dark."
There was command and warning in his tones.

▼▼▼

AFTER KEAH LEFT, Uxann made a quickie dinner of boiled cassava dumplings and buljohl with fresh milk to wash it down, and while eating, Paps gave her the inside scores about Keah. "Girl Chile, is like dis," he said. "You need some help around here. You's a schoolchile, and you does be working like man-wife. Ah can't let dat go so."

"Paps, you not having me doing nothing. I like to cook and keep house for you. What else I go do? I is your daughter."

"You is mih Girl Chile. Ah responsible for you. Ah have to make it nice for you. Dat's part why she coming."

"But what she go do, Paps? This house ent have dat much work, yu'know."

"Girl Chile, you is a good, good daughter. You better than dese common people 'round here. Is my place to let you show it," he said, his eye so serious on her that she flushed and looked away.

For a while, he picked his teeth with a sliver of cod-

fish bone. Then he went on, "And is business, anyhow.
She father owing me months now. And she mother is
yuh cousin, second cousin, so is kinda family, too. So
we agree to let she work off de debt part-time. Washing
some clothes, cooking dinner, and so on."

"Cooking dinner!" Uxann protested. "How you go
want she cooking we dinner, Paps?"

His eyes flickered away and, as if apologizing, he said,
"It'd only be a little while."

Except for the cooking, Uxann liked the idea. With
the notorious Keah in the house as guaranteed company, she'd hold an enviable position. Closest to the
newest and nastiest news, in school she'd get all the ears
of the morning's gossip. She said, "Paps, is okay, then.
I glad dat she here."

"You sure? Ah know she bad company for a girl like
you. But ah don't expect you to keep too close with her.
She not your type. She too young to be so hot."

"She not so bad, Paps. Is de boys and dem fault.
Harassing de girl all the time because she so pretty, and
. . . lively."

Paps looked at her sharply. "You just remember,
when she here, she working. She not your friend."

"But, Paps, if she here, I must talk to her. We does go
to school together, yu'know."

"Not anymore."

"Paps. What you saying? Look, I does be here all by

myself watching spirits in de house, while you galli-
vanting with your friends. I only too glad for de company. And after all, before dis thing happen with Keah,
we was good friends."

"Well, we'd see," Paps said. "I just don't want you
hanging around she while she doing her work. Remember she working for you."

▼▼▼

COME MONDAY MORNING in school, Uxann was the cen-
ter of attention. Just before they lined up for inspection,
some girls approached her, Eralee the direct spokes-
woman.

"Is it true Keah working servant for allyou?" she demanded.

"She not a servant," Uxann said. "She just helping
out in the evening."

"What she helping out with?"

"I don't know," said Uxann.

Gap-toothed Jainee, her hand as usual covering her
mouth, observed slyly, "I wonder what you'll be doing
when she helping out?"

Uxann looked at her coolly without answering, and

just then the bell rang to begin assembly, and the girls scattered to their positions on line. Eralee, of the same height and in the same class, going off with Uxann, said, "That no-teeth hag always getting into people business."

"And she always smelly, to boot," agreed Uxann.

Then they joined the silence of the lines.

▼▼▼

SCHOOL OVER, UXANN went directly home, eager to commence the new arrangement. She found the kitchen side door open top and bottom, and the consequent droppings from foraging fowl on the kitchen floor, but no Keah. Immediately peeved at the carelessness, she secured the bottom half of the door, then went to her room to hang up her book bag and change into home clothes. When she returned to the kitchen to clean the floor, Keah was there, sitting at the little table, smiling broadly. "I like dis place already, yu'know," she said.

Disarmed by the genuine smile, Uxann admitted, "Yes, it could be nice." Then continued, "But let me tell you right away. We can't leave the bottom doors open 'cause the fowls mess on the floor and stain it. And if Paps notice, is certain licks or long talk. So we have to be careful, okay?"

"Well, he can't lash me. I not he child. I only working for him," said Keah. Then, seeing Uxann's scowl begin, she added, "But ah wouldn't leave it open again."

Uxann gave her a sharp look and went to the outside kitchen for some fine ashes from the dirt oven. She well covered the three spots of fowl dung before sweeping the ash into the dustpan and tossing the mess into the yard. Then, with a damp floorcloth, she cleaned any remnants from the floor until there were no signs of the mess.

Throughout the operation, Keah never left the bentwood chair. And it was a miffed Uxann who went to start dinner.

It was to be bhagii and rice and chicken stewed down in coconut milk, and Uxann was in the garden picking the bhagii. After a while Keah wandered along. "What you want me to do?" she asked.

Still rankled, Uxann muttered, "I don't know. Whatever you feel." She continued picking.

"So where we going to cook, inside, or de outside kitchen?" Keah asked.

In her mind, Uxann retorted, Who's this "we" that cooking? Aloud, reluctantly, she said, "I does only cook inside when it raining."

"You want me to start de cooking fire, then?"

"If you want to."

And Keah left.

Anger and envy crowding back, Uxann glanced after her disdainfully. Keah's greasy hair was plaited to a simple braid and tied with a scrungy blue polka-dot ribbon at the nape of her neck. Her dress was a faded thing tight at the waist, and flaring over her wide hips—hips that switched up and down like a balance scale with her every step. All asudden, Uxann didn't want her there. She'd be a troublemaker. She wasn't clean, smelling of manure all the time, and she didn't look like she could cook water. Uxann sighed and gritted her teeth, feeling trapped and cheated of the best time of her every day, her time alone when she cooked for Paps. With sufficient bhagii, she returned morosely to the kitchen, determined to be uncooperative and unfriendly to her unwelcome help.

But in the kitchen, Keah had lit a nice hot fire, and had filled a bucket with clean water for vegetable washing and whatever, and was smiling a plea at Uxann under wet eyes just done crying. She said, "Uxann, don't treat me like stray dog. Right now, dis de only thing dat look like it have a chance to go right in mih life."

Uxann couldn't resist all that. "What stupidness you talking, girl," she said lightly. "I glad you here. Everything go be fine."

Together they made the meal, and when Seyeh came home, Uxann went and sat at the dining-room table with him as he wanted, while Keah brought the shared-out plates to the table, and sat for grace, and ate with them. The two girls were awkward with each other, and couldn't raise much conversation. Paps, smoky-eyed from how many he had tossed down, watched them thoughtfully, silent except for complimenting the meal. Afterwards, when Uxann helped take the plates and spoons to the kitchen, his glance was sharp, but not disapproving. Uxann returned to the table while Keah washed up.

The rattle and splash loud from the kitchen, Paps looked at her. "Wasn't too bad, huh?"

Uxann shrugged indifferently. "No."

"Right . . ." Then, getting up, he said, "Well, ah going in. Don't encourage she to stay when she finish, and do your homework when she gone."

"Yes, Paps," she answered dutifully. "Sleep nice."

And so said, so done. Almost. For so full and tiring was the day that Uxann drowsed off, and Keah had to wake her to say she was leaving.

SHE DIDN'T FEEL well since she woke up. Felt heavy, lethargic, as if sleep were a log that had rolled over her.

Halfway to school the dizziness started, once so strong she had to stoop down and steady herself by a hand to the rough ground until the giddy passed. By time she reached school it was blurry vision, unfocused anxiety, and a vague headache. She went to the office. Sister Marianne felt her for fever, looked in her eyes and down her throat, gave her pills, and sent her to sit in the quiet of the chapel. It would pass, she said. There, the pains began.

The first was like a hot spike into her lower guts, forcing a gasp; she bit her lip not to cry out as the pain gripped and diminished slowly, a reluctant thunder grumbling away down between her hips, an area that had never suggested pain before. Frightened, Uxann breathed deeply, building courage for a return to Sister Marianne. Then another pain hit, a stab like a pitchfork swung wild in her underbelly. She moaned in terror as the violence inside clenched longer, biting and wrenching and twisting. She curled up on the cool, hard bench, seeking to tighten herself into a knot of comfort or ease. But it didn't work. The pain slashed in again, stronger, more confident, reducing her to blubber and moan, confused and terrified. And worse upon bad news, a growing slickness in her knickers had her sniffing for the stink that would prove she'd dirtied herself with all her straining. That's when Sister Marianne found her.

It was her first period—the high point of embarrassment in her life, only prolonged as the nun, intending comfort, provided a clean cloth and showed her how to fold and place it to catch the flow, then went on and on with stuff that Uxann never heard, she so wanted to get to someplace private and hide her shame from the world.

Just before lunch recess, Sister Marianne set her free to go home. Focused by every eye they passed, the nun escorted her to class to get her book bag. Then, inner thighs a torture of chafing on the wadded cloth, Uxann minced down the steps of the side door, across the schoolyard, and into Nestor Road. She maintained the painful walk until, with a sharp lookabout, she was out of the school's sight. Then she stopped spread-legged, freeing the bulky pad away from her sore skin, and let the cool air soothe her. To improve the effect, she held her skirt wide and fanned gently.

Pain of cramps near forgotten, in a rhythm of a proper walk and pause from the agony, walk and pause, bit by bit, she headed to her shortcut through the forest. Once within that privacy, half-squatting so her legs spread until they did not rub, and feeling ridiculous but without the chafing sting, she waddled her way to her backyard.

Inside the house, she went to the WC, drew water, and laved her inner thighs clean of the sweat and seeped blood, wincing as she gentled the raw bruises dry. She took off her pants and examined the blood-soaked rag. Trembly that she was the source of the rust-dark splotch, she refolded the rag so it was narrower, then replaced it in the knickers' crotch and, shuddering slightly at the clammy touch, pulled the whole thing up on her.

She was dozing in bed, lying supine with legs apart, when Keah called, "Anybody home?"

"Yeeaahh . . ." she moaned, heaping great suffering on her tones. "Come in, de door open."

As hoped, Keah dashed in, wide-eyed. "What happen to you?" she asked.

"Is pain," whimpered Uxann, blinking and moving her head from side to side. "Pain . . ."

"Where? What happen?" Keah cried.

"I can't tell you the pain," Uxann mumbled, tears starting as Keah came over and sat on the bed's edge, smoothing Uxann's hair.

"Tell me anyhow," she said.

And, heart opened by her concern, Uxann poured out everything.

Her telling done, her sniffles gone, Uxann lay with her head on Keah's lap, relishing the comfort of her hair being smoothed and stroked. "Girl, I was so frighten," she said.

"It not so bad next time," said Keah.

"Next time? I have to go through this again?"

"Mmm-hmm, and many more, too. You better accustom yourself to de idea."

"But it does hurt so much."

"Dat's because it was de first. Mine was bad first time, too. But dey got better later," said Keah.

"But why it have to hurt at all, huh? Why?"

"Well, yu'know what my mother tell me. She say dat way back in 'Nancy story times when thing like dat used to happen, womankind wanted to wear gold and try to trick the moon for de secret of how to make jewel from light. But when de moon fool she back, womankind get vex and curse de moon. What she didn't know was dat King Sun was de moon child, and he don't like anybody mistreating he mother. So when he hear about womankind behavior, he suffer this revenge on she, that every time de moon belly full, womankind must bear de pain and bleed. So pain and blood is we birthright until age make we wise."

"Is so it happen?" Uxann asked.

"Is what mih mooma tell me."

"Well, girl, I wish I was old already," said Uxann.

"Well, not me, girl. I want to be young till ah dead. With dey no teeth and grumpy self, I don't notice old people being so happy 'bout anything."

Then Keah turned the talk practical, telling Uxann about easing cramps: of how to brew tender orange leaves, and how to boil cotton buds, and the aloe-and-egg brew to clean out the body afterwards. Uxann listened drowsily until Keah, noticing, suggested she rest and let her cook dinner. Gratefully, Uxann closed her eyes, and immediately was in a deep sleep, never waking up until next morning.

▼▼▼

THEY WERE IN the kitchen, engrossed, Keah on the chair, running gossip as she picked at jiggers between her toes, Uxann, big spoon in hand, tending over a pot of stewing duck. "Oh, God, dat food smelling good!" Keah exclaimed.

"In ten minutes it ready," said Uxann.

"Ten minutes. Well, I telling yuh, my mouth ready already."

"Girl, your mouth—"

"WHAT THE HELL YUH DOING? EH? EH?" Seyeh's raging voice thundered from the doorway.

Frozen guilty in their places, they stared at each other. Uxann started explanations: "I was just checking on de pot for she. . . ."

Eyes mad red, Paps strode over and slapped her as his rum breath blasted, "And you ready to lie, too. Lie for she, eh. What ah tell you? Not dat she working for you? And here you be, playing cook while she pickin' she foot. And you ready to lie for she!" He smacked her face again. "Get out mih sight!" he shouted.

Uxann, face burning more from embarrassment, but holding back her tears, walked stiffly to her room and slammed the door behind her, then reopened it slightly so she could listen.

Keah was in a trouble pot, she knew, and worried more because she had put her there. Drink rogued Seyeh, made him mean and violent. She heard him now, voice lower, but still angrily going on at Keah, asking questions one after another, too fast to accept any answer. Just hammering the questions hard on the poor girl, nailing her down.

There came a quiet, then a giggle from Keah, weak, pacifying, more whimper than glee. Then the clang of a replaced pot-cover. She had probably stirred the pot. Paps' voice came again, still vexed, but nearer normal, instructing Keah. Then the stomp as he left the kitchen. Swiftly and softly, as he came past to his room, Uxann closed her door.

Two, three minutes later, she opened to Keah's stealthy knock.

She carried a plate of food. "He say you stay in your room. An' you eating dinner in here rest of de week." She kept her voice low, her eyes edgy at the door. "He say we too stubborn, so de ban is how you must pay. An' since he can't hit me, I must carry all de cooking burden."

Uxann took the plate, put it on her bed. "Is all right, I could take it. But he was really vex. I didn't even hear him coming in. Long time I ent seen him so crazy." Reminded of the slaps, her hand went to her smarting face. "How it looking?"

Keah examined close. "It a little puffy, little red, but not too bad. It should go down by morning. I'll bring a wet cloth for you to cool it. But quick. He waiting."

"Thanks, Keah. I sorry I get you in all this mess," said Uxann.

Keah grinned and shrugged. "Is not your fault. Ah bring it on myself, too." She smiled perfect whites and sneaked out the door, closing it quietly.

Uxann soothed her face for a while, but gradually the smell of the hot food was too enticing, so she settled herself on the bed and ate.

Afterwards, it was homework, and then sleep. Her last thought before dropping off was that although sometimes she couldn't stand how slim and pretty she was, Keah was indeed her best friend.

▼▼▼

FRIDAY, LAST DAY of the ban, the school bell dismissed to a race against threatening clouds. The air was heavy, grey, with an acrid gunpowder smell. Not too distant, a restive giant thunder rumbled and grumbled and rolled the loaded clouds. It wasn't long before they'd burst. Still on the public road, anxious eye on the lowering sky, Uxann walked properly, conscious of how fat people looked clumsy when they hurried, but longed for the privacy of her forest-track shortcut, where she could burst out running all speed, and perhaps beat the rain home.

She got to the break from the graveled road as the first big drops splattered down, pelting hard as pellets, one stinging her eye as she looked skywards before jumping the storm drain to get under the forest's canopy. No raindrops were there yet, although the growing patter overhead promised soon. But now, safe in her forest, she could cut swift tracks.

When she came out of the forest to the last stretch home through the abandoned grass field, it seemed she'd beat the major downpour. It was drizzling steadily, though. Her legs were slicked the instant she started through the glistening, half-flattened grass. Swift-moving waves of fine rain gusted over her. Head to the wind, eyes slitted against the spray, Uxann held her book bag to her bosom and aimed her run for the backyard gate—even as she realized it wouldn't make a difference, that a dousing was for certain. Even as the lightning struck, frying the heavy air, sizzling to the ground not twenty yards in front. Uxann stopped stock-still, her half-blinded gaze jerked skywards. She stared, her slowly clearing vision filled with the Gabilan.

His perch was the skeleton of a burned-out hog-plum tree. A frequent lightning victim, it had stood there for several years blackly reaching at heaven, the thinner uppermost branches bare as charcoal, while along its trunk and robust lower branches parasite vines flourished upwards. On one spare, lofty bastion, the king of hawks poised looking down on her, black wings halfway furled, ready but resting, threat of its cruel, golden eyes fixing hard into Uxann's mind and heart. Trapped in the gaze like a mouse, enthralled and trembling, she submitted. Then an awful thunder ripped apart the streaming sky, splintering showers down on her. And Gabilan was gone.

Dazed, feeling a pilgrim's anguish, she found herself trudging the last bit home, almost at the kitchen garden's bamboo fence. The dreadful eyes of Gabilan flashed through her mind again, and set her shuddering. The yellow beams had pierced right through her, seeking into her deepest secret close. It could bear no good when Gabilan looked on you like that. But why her? What had she done to be so persecuted? Suddenly woeful, she panicked through the rowed vegetable beds as if chased, ploughing a beeline of destruction through their well-tended neatness, and burst into the kitchen.

She paused to regain composure, then slowly realized

a muddy river was dripping on the floor. She roughed off the sneakers, and stripped down the drenched clothes right there and bundled all into the sink. Then she noticed a half-eaten mango in a saucer on the counter, and realized somebody was home. Assuming Paps, she started for her room to dry off and dress. Hand on the knob, pushing her door open, she heard Paps scream, "Oh, God! You so sweet . . ."

It was a scream all at once so tender and helpless and happy that, as if her will were quicksand, Uxann stood like stone, the tones sinking into her.

Not that she hadn't heard him with women before. Always, though, it had been vague, away, distant sounds. Because, feeling shy and intrusive when he had a woman in the house, she normally remained in her room, or outside, disappeared and noiseless. But this cry. . . !

"Aiieee!" A gasp and his sigh, carefree, boyish, puzzlingly familiar, reminded she was eavesdropping. So she entered her room and softly closed Paps' business away.

To the rattle of rain on the galvanized roof, a comforting sound encouraging dreams without sleep, Uxann dried herself. Snatches of thought surfaced and slipped off like fish nibbling bait. Nap time was nigh. She was pulling her housedress over her head when it came to her: The tone of Paps' cry was the same as the

boys' those dusky evenings they troubled girls at the
standpipe. The connection tugged out a small smile,
which quickly turned to pursed lips of concern. That
he'd be done with the loudness betimes Keah arrived,
she worried.

But then she lay down and nodded off.

▼▼▼

SHE DREAMT A dream of something that really happened: One time some tourist people who had run out
of road blundered into the village in their Land-Rover,
trying to find the spring that started the big river. Because he was the estate overseer, the villagers brought
them to Paps in the rumshop, half-drunk and out for
fun. Talking patois, he bet the villagers he could make
the tourists give him money, make pappyshow of
them. Then he began telling the tourists how important and rare the village was. And that he was the
mayor. (Him naked-back, barefoot, with a glass of
rum in his hand.) He picked out Bohra's sad-eyed
seven-year-old girlchild, and told her to stand with a
bucket of water balanced on her head. Then he told
the tourists the child had asked for a picture. They

were only too happy to take out their fancy cameras, and soon snapshots were coming out ready-made, darkening to true colours as they were held in hand. Then the tourists gave Paps an instant picture of himself, which pleased him so, he told them long stories about wars and kings and criminals that no one had ever heard before. It got even better when, in patois, he asked the villagers to act out parts of his story, and they began prancing about, dropping as dead in the hot sun playing warriors, or whatever. The tourists, excited by all this bacchanal, took pictures like mad, then passed out money and chewing gum. Then finally, pretending it was the way to the starter spring, Paps gave them directions to the main road and sent them off. As they happily drove away, the village folk took in with an extreme case of laughing sickness, howling how Paps was a jackass, meaning he was clever and brave; the men feting Paps in the rumshop, the women smiling back to their humdrum, the young folk who got lucky trying to blow bubbles with chewing gum.

In Uxann's dream, the twist to the story was: All while the foolery was going on, an older-man tourist with a short dark beard kept sliding bright, private eyes at Uxann. And gradually, somehow his eyes changed to a wise and wicked golden stare, a yellow beam that stripped her naked, went right through her like she was

candle wax. Dark in the middle of her belly, brooding
and gloomy, he could see the sly demon in her who
wanted to show off everything to his nasty, one-minded
focus on her fancy. And what was she doing? Shamed
and queasy, yet grateful, she was exposing for his
greedy eye.

She woke sharply from the dream with a strange tension, her belly crawling with gooseflesh. Next thing she
heard was Keah singing in the kitchen. Which suddenly
stopped and turned to a "Damn!" Then a muttering,
and a scraping of pots, and a slosh of re-washing. This
cleared away her disturbance, and set Uxann musing on
a cheery thought. Today was the last of banned quality
meals.

The days they'd worked together had taught Uxann
one thing. Whatever she was, Keah wasn't a kitchen
person. She could fly gossip like a chatter-bird. She
could make life funny like a baby monkey. She could
sing. She could dance. She was pretty. But she
couldn't cook. She left dirt on the vegetables. Plates
slipped and broke when she washed them. She never
salted the pot. In a kitchen, Keah was good company.
But whatever her food, be it rice or meat or ground
provisions, the common flavour was burnt pot bottom.

Just then, re-born from the kitchen came Keah's song,
testing at first before bursting lightheartedness right

through the house. Caught by the cheer, Uxann smiled for her friend.

▼▼▼

AFTER THE BAN was served, they made a simple arrangement. Uxann cook, Keah lookout! They were strict at it, mutual dread of Seyeh motivating their efficiency high. And the strategy worked. At the dinner table, food was mouth-watering tasty again, although, strangely, conversation dried up. Even the private eyes and smirks that their top-secret trick was going so well became stale.

Uxann recalled the dinner table before Keah. It used to be a talkative time of day, Seyeh always discussing the village, expounding his idea that the village as a whole was like a child—growing and learning, passing through good and bad times, gradually maturing. He pointed out his part as leader, overseer. Told her why he had put up their concrete-and-brick house with running water and inside toilet. The end was nigh for tapia and thatch, he told her. Those temporary houses must be shed like baby teeth. He had to set example.

Seyeh knew everybody's business, and Uxann missed hearing him mauvais-langue the jiggers in the young village's feet. At those dinner chats, he used to treat her like a big person, talking straight, naming names, sometimes even cussing. Now, with Keah around, he played the role of a regular father. Asked her what she had learned in school, what she thought of this or that. Before Keah, she never had to think. All to do was give her ears, and a hearty laugh every time he cracked a joke.

So gradually, Uxann developed an escape course in her dinner habits. Eyes to her plate, she'd eat steadily until done, then excuse herself to the toilet and brush her teeth. Then back to the table for "Good night, Paps!" and "Until tomorrow, Keah." Then to her room for her homework and sleep. In there, off and on, there'd be a tidbit of whatever of dinner had tasted special, her put-aside treat once the cooking had been done.

Sometimes, from her room, she'd hear Keah clearing the table and washing up before the back door creaked her out. Sometimes she'd follow Paps' tread out of the kitchen and into the hiss of the dewed grass as he went to check on the animals. Sometimes, absorbed in books, or thoughts, or sleep, she heard nothing at all.

▼▼▼

THE SOUND OF the toilet flushing awoke her to the morning. Puzzled, Uxann listened to the sound, shaping it to a water droplet, small but growing, then big and rounded as the toilet door opened and closed after the flush, the rushing water growing small again before a smooth-point stop. Unusual was that Paps used the toilet. Rain or shine, morning come, his habit was to pee in the banana stool in the backyard. But her bladder was calling her, too. So she got up and went to begin her morning routines.

First after the toilette was to drink a big cup of water. Recently in school, she'd heard a girl, looking the proof, say this kept the skin clear and the weight down.

Beauty care done, next was the morning fire. She arranged some kindling from under the fireside in the middle of the coalpot, then ringed this with chunks of charcoal until they were crowding over the kindling. Through a hole in the can's cork, she carefully leaked a few drops of kerosene onto the kindling. Finally, she lit a match to the pile and watched as it sootily caught fire.

The brimstone of the struck match, the kerosene like rotting sugarcane, the clean blue wood smoke— the varied smells assailed and made her morning fully risen. Tasting the burnt sulphur tang of the blackened matchhead, she put on a pot of water to heat, and went out into the yard to gather whatever eggs the fowl had laid.

An hour later she had eaten the morsel her latest diet allowed and was dressed in uniform ready for school. Paps had never come out, so she assumed he might've been drunk last night. Satisfied with a final look in the toilet's mirror, she shouted into the house the usual "I gone, Paps!" There was no acknowledgment as she left through the kitchen side door. But she had expected none.

▼▼▼

TODAY WAS INSPECTION day; no shortcut to school for Uxann, fearing for her whitened sneakers getting dirtied from the forest track. But, started early enough, it was pleasant walking the long way, enjoying the chirpy birds and the cool, pre-sunshine breeze. Rain had fallen last night, although the graveled road was already dry, and the morning was quiet as if freshly woken by the aroma of orange blossoms in the air. With every move, the starched stiffness of her clothes made her feel like a letter in a neat envelope of school uniform. Heavy though she was, she felt she looked good.

Their zebu bull muddying the storm drain, Roonee and her scrawny little brother rode up and past her—most likely taking the animal to their parents' rice paddy. Popular in school, Roonee and her brother had the reputation for mischief. As if practicing at it, the boy had straddled the bull backwards and, with a gleeful grin, was watching whence he'd come. Their bare feet were muddy, although they, too, were in best clothes; Uxann knew exactly how rank the uniforms would smell later on in class. Even at this safe distance, she wrinkled her nose as she waved at them. "See you in school," they shouted back, all smiles and laughter.

▼▼▼

It DIDN'T TAKE long—lining up in classes after the in-spection—before Uxann felt it: that they were talking about her. And automatically she fled into herself. As she nearly caught each fleeting eye, as her passage quelled each whispering group, she assumed a contained smile, a blank nonseeing gaze, a poised carriage, all expressing her chosen aloofness. Behind her certain face, though, consternation churned. The straw of confusion: How was she the butt this time?

She pleaded belly pains to the nuns at afternoon recess and was released to a doleful walk home. She watched her footsteps meeting the gravel, the powder-white sneakers all asudden seeming to glare back at her. It came to her that popular Roonee, like most others, went barefoot in school, their shoes being only for Sunday mass. When she was little, Uxann went to church head to toes in white. Hat, ribbons, dress—usually with a flare skirt, long socks, and shoes. Soft white leather shoes with silver buckles. Paps used to polish them with snake oil to keep them supple and soft for his baby girl's chubby feet. She was a favorite then. Everyone was close. They hugged. They laughed. They said how pretty she was.

A groan of rending pain interrupted—that near-human screech when the wind scrapes big branches against each other, and as always it tugged a sympathetic wince from her. She noticed nearby the entrance to an unfamiliar forest track, hardly used from the way the bush was reclaiming the opening. A swift glance around. No one about. And on impulse, she jumped the drain and crashed the front bush into the track. Didn't need but feel that the last of the starch in her skirt was damp. Didn't need a look that the too-white sneakers were dirtied now. She took them off and stuffed their dismay into the school bag. Then, furrowing her toes into the moist leafy floor, she set off through the woods.

Gradually, the forest became friendly to her, fitted her in. One cicada, then another, shrilled their claims. Just out of sight, the birds resumed with cheeps and chatter. Butterflies—a big blue one, a grey eyespot on yellow wings, a tiny busy greeny—fluttered zigzag in and out of her vision. Sunrays and light shafts flickered and shifted along the ground and off leaves trembling from teasing breezes. The rhythm of it, from the pad of her footfall to the thump of her heart, she felt in.

She roamed aimlessly. Ranged upon a promising tamarind tree. Saw a zangee strike a coscarob. Squatted and peed on a bachac nest. All the while, though, her feet well made way, and she eventually found herself on the opposite side of the abandoned grass field near home. About to leave the forest track, she saw a figure start across the open space—from the direction of her house. Automatically, she hid and waited for a better view. He soon came clear: Preddy Dassen. Uxann smiled wryly, feeling relieved and wise. Dog learn to suck egg and can't stop, she mused. Now she figured she knew what the gossip in school was about.

▼▼▼

Uxann put up her books, changed into house clothes, and went in search of Keah, intending to lord her knowledge. She wasn't hard to find, her singing coming from the side of the house where the outside pipe was. Clothes-washing was done in a large metal tub raised up on four cement bricks. The extra height brought the tub's rim to waist level and made it comfortable when using the scrub board. With the water just pouring down into the tub, washing clothes had lost its hardest toil, bringing water from the standpipe—a major reason why many women washed right at the spout's mouth, or on a stony spot at the edge of the river. Of her required chores, Keah seemed to like it most. Or maybe tolerate was nearer.

She was working to a catchy tune with a quick beat, using splash for rhythm, scrubbing and plunging the clothes into the bubbling water in time, and grinning like a child playing splatterfall. She hardly wrung the clothes at all to hang them, just hoisted each piece, draining its small torrent, to the clothesline and pinned it there, still trickling. With smiling eye at the flow on the ground,

Uxann greeted, "Like river coming down, or what?"

Keah turned, happy-faced. "What ah go do? I not strong, mih hands soft. I can't wring clothes," she said, laughing and raising up her slim, silver-bangled arms.

What caught Uxann's attention, though, was how the water had plastered Keah from head to foot. Polka-dot ribbon tying away one of her thick, dripping braids. Dingy bodice—old school uniform—soaking wet, stuck on her body, breasts made plain naked, black nipples like cherry pits. As for lower down, clearer than decent Uxann could see the black hairs sticking from her panties through the soaking, faded blue cloth.

Uxann turned her eyes away, flushing as she recalled her first intent to needle about Preddy. But now, mindful that he had just sneaked away from a Keah so all-revealing, and reminded of their "raid" on Dosaro's, Uxann saw that raising the topic at all would probably get much further than comfortable. So, with a mind to let sucking-egg dogs lie, she went back into the house.

As was their compromise arrangement, Uxann set the pots to cook, alerted Keah to watch them well, then went to her room. When Paps came home, she was there doing homework, Keah in the kitchen cooking. Later at the dinner table, everybody was happy with a tasty, well-cooked meal. Uxann felt even better as she noticed that Keah had brought and changed into dry, sensible clothes. Afterwards, she said her good-nights,

brushed her teeth, and, with a big cup of water for the
night, went to sleep.

▼▼▼

A NICE SATURDAY nearing midday. Uxann had returned
from a fruitful trip to the orchard. No cheap, skulking
Mr. Dosaro. No slips or falls while climbing. No prickles in the hands. No eyes that saw. No unpleasantness at
all. She unloaded her skirt and bag, and assessed her
spoils. This time it was mainly cymites, sugar apples,
and a few mangoes. Of the mangoes, a doux-doux and
a john would go to Paps—his preference, since he dis-
liked the gum on his lips from cymite and the extra
sweet of sugar apple.

She put the fruit in a cupboard away from the flies,
and roamed into the rest of the house possessively.
Catching a yen to make it spic and span, she was soon
putting whatever in its place, touching here a chair,
fixing there a curtain. In the toilet, she washed the bowl,
scrubbed the shower curtain, and polished the sink mirror, the only one in the house. Not so much needed, the
clean-up action returned the place to her, at least on
weekends, when Keah didn't come. Eventually, content

with the state of grace inside, she donned rubber boots and went out to nurture the kitchen garden.

Time after—late afternoon—putting cow dung around the young pepper plants to protect them from crawling pests, Uxann was startled by a crash from the house—the kitchen, from the potlike clang. Figuring a pullet had got in, she clumped her tall-tops to attend it. Peering in, she found Paps, home from the rumshop, drunk as a fish. Uxann sucked her teeth. He was leaning, half-lying on the counter next to the sink, and seemed fast asleep except for one eye twisted open by the pressure against the metal drainboard, giving him a confused, funny look. Despite herself, it drew a giggle. Oh, Paps, she thought, you barely made it home.

She kicked off the boots, went in, and shook his shoulder firmly. "Paps! Get up! Wake up, Paps!"

His staring lizard eye rolled lazily. An elastic dribble drooled from his lips.

She leaned close to his ear. "The cow, Paps. The cow gone straying."

That roused him up to a stagger. "Where? Wha—? Wha—?" he slurred, grabbing the sink for balance as his red, rolling eyes searched about the kitchen stupidly.

Now that he was upright, Uxann held him by the waist and stumbled him towards his room. "You'd better sleep it off, Paps." He staggered off. She returned to the kitchen to undo the disarray.

A few minutes later she heard him slam into the toilet. Going to the door, she was about to ask if he was all right when there came the longest stream of pee she'd ever heard, then a ripping *f-o-o-o-p-s,* so drawn out and meandering, she collapsed in silent laughter and crawled back to the kitchen on her knees.

The toilet remained quiet so long that Uxann finally went back to check. She knocked on the closed door, at first questioningly, then insistently firm. No answer. "Paps?"

Silence.

She opened the door and peeked in. Seyeh was slumped forward on the toilet seat, head on arms folded across his knees, seeming dead again. She slammed the door shut, then again. A few seconds passed, and she peeked once more. He was swaying but afoot, his boxer shorts tugged up askew, although decent enough.

Wrinkling her nose against the various body and waste odors, she crowded into the toilet to grasp him about the waist and guide him out. Patient with his rubber-legged walk, his arm as if for life around her neck, she wrestled him along the short hallway to his room. He began a fretful mumbling she couldn't follow—something about leaving him alone, although he kept his arm locked about her neck. She sat them on the bed's edge and leaned back, hoping he'd fall limp on the bed. But he would not release her neck, just hung there clumsily, twisting her skin, she was sure, to a bruise. In exasperation, she cried, "Let me go and lie down, Paps!"

Then, clear from his stupid mumbling, in that coaxing boyish tone that had fascinated her, Paps said, "So you want lie down again, huh? Gul Keah, you too hot, yu'know. But you so sweet, too."

Instantly angry and stronger than needed, Uxann shoved him off her like he was a bag of snakes.

Limp on the bed, he was mumbling again: "No . . . tomorrow when she gone . . . not now, doux-doux . . . I tired."

His meaning flashed a squeezing pain from mind to heart or belly or that place marrow-deep where only comfort belonged. Keah, her best friend! He was doing it to Keah.

He was back to his drunken mumbling, plain only at calling her name: "Keah, Keah . . ."

Without intent or understanding why, Uxann answered, "Yes, Seyeh?" thrilling as she mimicked Keah's pliant molasses voice.

But he just curled up on his side and groaned something as, with disgust, she looked down at him reduced to baby size by the big bed. Stiffened with rage, she jerked the coverlet over him and left the room.

Mind unfocused, she returned to the kitchen and prepared a quick, lonely dinner, which she ate without tasting. Then, with night descending, she took care of

the animals, closing pen gates, putting out feed and water, securing some baby chicks. But these normally rest-
ful chores left her still unsettled, the knowledge of Keah
and Paps deviling her peace of mind. She tried to do
schoolwork but, as the words just blurred black on the
pages, gave up on it until the morrow. Finally, deciding
to sleep on it, she changed into her bag of a nightdress,
did her toilette, and drank a glass of water.

Sleep wouldn't come, though. Behind too tightly
shut eyes, the ghostlike idea of Paps and Keah smoth-
ered peace. It set her staring through the dark of the
room listening to night; all calm except for the come-
and-go rustle of a questing breeze. A quavery crow of
some rooster came floating by from afar. The setting
hen in the box by the kitchen window clucked. A goat
sneezed. The breeze provoked the leaves again. Then,
in the house, a sudden snore from Paps ganged them
back into her mind; him with Keah, bulling dog and
bitch in heat. Uxann squirmed on the mattress, sleep
all asudden hostile, until, unable to bear it, she rose
from the antsy bed. A walk in the cool night would
perhaps soothe.

Her dry throat drew her to the pitcher in the kitchen;
a mouthful might help. But every sip tasted of their
betrayal, and refreshed how amiss they were, and didn't
at all slow the swirl of the mess in her mind. So she
dropped the calabash in the sink, unlatched the kitchen

door top and bottom. Under the quiet trees, the big night, the deep, deep sky, she drifted about the yard feeling crossed and anxious.

A departing flutter, a cheated "hoot-hoot" came almost atime with a raucous squawk as, close overhead, a startled chicken regained its perch after the hungry snatch of an owl. An echo of the incident thrummed her mind. They were as cruel, and got away with it! An injustice that hammered her feelings and sent her stumbling down the yard, until, passing the pen, a promise in the warm, peaceful cow smell caught and drew her in. And there, down on the strewn fodder between the safe cows, she curled herself up in her muddle.

▼▼▼

NOISES, MOVEMENT, PERHAPS the cows, roused her some while after, and she set off to her proper bed. As she returned through the kitchen door, a mighty snoring met her, which wasn't the reason her feet turned to his room. She opened the door slowly to see him—on his back, slack-jawed, sleep roaring furious from the gape of his mouth.

Softly she prowled about the unfamiliar room, pulled

here and there by envy and despair. Maybe Keah had sat on that chair, pulled it to the little table, opened its drawer. Or handled his water jug, drunk from his glass. All intimacies she, Uxann, his flesh and blood, had been denied. All insults that had lessened her. She looked back at him snoring in the dimness, and a tumult seized her, a yen to cause him discomfort, to make him wake up morning-come unslept and sore, in some way make him share her distress.

Skidding her eyes from the ugly humour, she glimpsed a barely remembered trunk in the far corner from the bed. Bold in the rush, she swung open the lid and poked through, turning about the musty-smelling stuff in it—rough cloth, stacked papers, folders, and, near the bottom, some fabric that was smooth and soft. She pulled it out, a dress, red even in the vague light. It was satin or silk. Measured against her body, it was far too small. She held it to her face, liking the slippery, flimsy cool. There was a scent to it, too, a persistent hint of fragrance beyond the fusty trunk smell. She breathed in deeply through nose and mouth, trying to filter more of the aroma into her, to capture it. And suddenly a memory rushed forward: Outside was pelting rain and thunder and lightning and screams telling trouble and torment. Inside the house—their first one, the two-room, dirt-floor, mud-walled, regular village house—inside was only ugly tension. At the window, toddler-she had flapped the corner of a dingy curtain, and was peeping at the woman outside. A woman naked in the rain. A woman weeping and pleading, long wet hair snarled black about her face and shoulders, trying to cover her fancy with her hands. It was her mother—her naked mother shamed and cowering in the pelting rain. Her mother's eyes begging the house. Shaking her head like she bazodie. Her mouth sagged and drooling, bawling like a cow. And at the door of the house was Paps, cutlass in hand, barring the way, closing off shelter, with his face hard, his eyes shining like the clean edge of the threatening steel he stood firmly planted with.

Clear through the memory, Uxann felt his harsh determination. Never would he forgive the woman, her mother. Never would he let her back in.

Her own shudder and the wet of her tears on the slippery cloth brought her back. Quieting her sniffles, she re-folded and replaced the dress in the trunk. Where was her mother now? This dress was probably all Uxann had of her. And he had it closed away in his smelly trunk. Bitterness crept her over to look close at Seyeh, now scrunched up like a sick puppy at a nipple. Mr. Hard Bad Man who put out her mother.

She sat on the edge of the bed and, with reckless spite, smacked the back of his head. He grunted briefly, but hadn't felt it good enough. She smacked his head even harder. He grunted, rolled over, and curled up on the other side. As she was about to smack him again, something spotted black sticking out from under the pillow narrowed her eye. She drew it out and held it closer: It was Keah's other blue polka-dot ribbon.

New rage flared. So the beast in heat had her stuff everywhere, like she was living in the house! Uxann flung the ribbon away and scrubbed her hand against her nightdress. Maybe while she was in school, both of them were here doing it every day. Suddenly suspicious, she went and pulled open the table drawer. The bottle of rum there was more than half-empty. And it all added up. What she had noticed on Keah's breath lately was a rummy smell. Seyeh was turning her into a drinker, although she didn't carry the same scent as he. Hers was sweeter, more like old molasses. Curious, Uxann uncorked the bottle, whiffed, then took a swig. Raw in her mouth, even when swallowed away, it left a burn. Tasted terrible, but for a soothing warmth after it left her mouth. She took another tentative gulp, then another, which sealed that she didn't like it, and would never crave liquor. Then she corked the bottle and replaced it. Hot from her stomach, rushing to her neck, she felt a flush from the rum right away. So, this was how his life was, eh? she mused, squinting at him lying there wheezing like an old billy goat. After preaching how she was too hot, here he was making Keah into a rummy like him, so he could bull her. He was another dribbling dog, tongue hanging out, just like all those boys in school who trailed after Keah, always trying for a chance to rub up against her skinny body and do it.

In a fury, she climbed up on the bed and grabbed hold of his arm and pinched, hard. Paps groaned and weakly pulled away. She pinched again, nearer the shoulder, her fingers slipping off the drum-tight skin. It got through some, though, for he brushed his hand at her, and gathered and shifted himself onto his back, the slack jaw lending him a foolish, surprised look. She wished in spite that his workers should see him so. At the same time a dizziness took her, and it occurred to her that he was so drunk to the world, she could do anything to him. Partly to steady herself, partly so she could look down on his stupid face, Uxann straddled Seyeh's belly. Then she slapped his face. He groaned and tossed his head to the other side, and brought his arm up to ward away attack. "Not now, Keah," he mumbled. "Ah tired, doux-doux. Not now."

A pang of jealousy, of anguish, overwhelmed her. Drunk or sober, sleep or wake, all he could think about was doing it with Keah—skinny, bold-faced Keah! Swirling purple, raw, and mighty, blood and madness filled her head. Passion, ugly and vengeful, caught her up, wrenching anxieties from her, twisting tears out as she swooned. "Paps . . . Keah? . . ." she whimpered,

stretching herself full over Seyeh, hugging on him, holding tight for longing . . .

▼▼▼

. . . MIDDLE OF THE night she woke up startled, reaching
about, feeling the wrongness of the bed. She touched
him aside her, and it all rushed back like a whirlpool.
Bringing Paps to bed. Prowling the room. The dress.
The rum. Her rage. Shamefaced, she recalled slapping
him about, her ugly intentions. Then after that her rum-
headed swoon. Mouth sour and dry as ashes, trembling
at how terrible she had been, she slid off the bed, pulling
down her nightshift, which had worked up to her navel.
There was a thick slickness high between her legs. In-
vestigating, her hand touched wet at her fancy. She
wiped at it with her shift, and turned to flee the room,
nearly stumbling over the coverlet on the floor. As she
threw the cover over Paps sleeping curled up as if
cold, she cringed shy at the sight of his wrinkled thing
hanging limp out of his shorts. But the bending down
and effort of tossing the cover had sent her mind reel-
ing again, so, hands to the steady wall, walking a heel-
to-toe roll not to creak the floorboards, she escaped his

room, closed the door, and staggered back to her own.

▼▼▼

WHEN SHE AWOKE Sunday morning, her head felt like a balloon swollen tight nearly to the burst of pain. After the first start out of her restless sleep, every move was made deliberately, with careful head poised as if it were a brimming bucket on her neck.

She set about her normal routines: morning toilette, build the fire, wash the troughs, milk the goats and zebus, loose and chase them to their wandering, feed the fowl—all the regular weekend morning chores before she got to making lunch. And in the easy pace of these familiars, she soothed her mind to reason and relax.

Mid-afternoon, Seyeh stumbled out to the banana stool in the backyard, and at her usual seat in the inside kitchen, Uxann felt her heart trip. In front of her on the table was dessert, a ripe guava. A buzz around it said sour flies, but Uxann was uncaring. Through the back window, she gazed blindly at the outside kitchen, listening to Paps' progress. Forward on her left, through the side window, she glimpsed him passing to the standpipe. Then came the splashing as he washed, her heart pounding harder and faster as she waited for the end of it. A house fly buzzed the sour flies away and set claim on the guava. Uxann shooed it away automatically, the echo of her thumping heart a hammer in her head.

She had picked up the guava and reached it to her mouth when Paps poked his head through the opened top half of the kitchen door, moustache dripping frothy around his mouth, hair still draining onto his shoulders. He was brushing his teeth with a hand's length of hibiscus stem. "Mornin', Girl Chile," he said. "Ah tellin' yuh straight, ah feeling stale drunk for a sailor fleet. Mih head in pain. Is as if ah come second in a giant stickfight."

Uxann put down the guava unbitten, went to the earthen pitcher, drew a glass of water, and sipped it.

Paps spat frothy saliva into the yard and looked back at her sharply, his white, frayed-topped hibiscus stem grasped like a pencil in a puzzled pupil's hand. Sudden sorry around him like a cloud, he sucked his teeth and shook his head. "So what ah do dis time dat you so vex with me?" he said.

Through her frontal view, Uxann gazed serenely at the outside kitchen. At the corner of her eye, though, she caught his apologetic manner, and a rhythm of relief bounded into her heartbeat: He didn't remember her attack. He thought it was *he* who had misbehaved. She turned and looked at him straight. "Is rum beat you, Paps," she said, "same as again. All de time you say it yourself. In any battle, HardRum will beat Strongman. But you still acting like you young. These days you not even knowing what happen when you drink. Soon people'll be talking about you. . . ."

This gush of real concerns filled her eyes, and choked off her plaint. A deep in-breath to contain the flood, then, with arms folded across her chest, she turned her face from him.

Paps sucked his teeth again, shook a morose head, and slowly went from the window.

Uxann didn't feel sorry for him at all.

▼▼▼

A SUNSET-SADDENED EVENING, horizon weepy red, deeper up the sky darkened bruised purple. A thin gold blade of new moon hung poised there, though already yielding to the grouping blue-black promises of midnight rain. The gloomy sky well fit Uxann's mood, a half-week now glum weather had. Today, coming from school, she started off dinner as usual. Except that, not wanting her company, she'd left Keah with the stirring while she went to tend the animals. At which she took deliberate time.

The last few days, now alerted, she was discovering a brand-new side of helpmate Keah. All afternoon she'd present her usual happy-go-lucky self, but as soon as Paps got home, she'd turn other-faced like a penny. No sharp remarks at all. Broad-mouth laughter switched to drop-eyed titters. And for every proper thing she did, a glance to Paps. A bent-neck glance that carried common yard scenes, like a duck cocking tail for a drake, or a pullet squatting one-sided for the rooster. Amazed at these changes, Uxann could scarcely believe. Keah! So melting and patient? Docile like a cow? Always with a simper for Seyeh? Hot-mouth Keah, who always had a pepper spike for answer, who could stare down a needle.

Case in point: Halfway through dinner, Paps paused eating and remarked, "A squeeze of lime would go down well on this boiled cassava, huh?" "Lime" barely out of his mouth, Keah was flashing from the table, then back with slice in hand. Paps snapped her a look, while Uxann, eyes to her own plate, pretended not to notice. Keah went the long way around the table to give him the lime, and in returning to her place, although there was room behind Paps' chair for a jackass to dance, she still managed to lightly touch his shoulder. Helpless as a shudder, he flinched and, as Keah sat, sent a stiff eye at her satisfied face.

All of which, while poking the fried bodie beans and onions to yet another quadrant of her plate, Uxann well observed from under her lowered lids.

Soon fed up to her neck, and to depart their open game, she said good-nights and left the table. Did her toilette, and took her cup of water back to her room for sipping through homework. Which was a two-part grind. First about a trundle of trains that started at different times going several places at varied speeds, and she was supposed to cypher time schedules out of this maze. Then was a puzzle of maps, Mercator and otherwise, on which she had to place rivers, cities, and resources.

She managed them, though, got lost in the effort, and, when finished tired, slept.

▼▼▼

NOT KNOWING EXACTLY why, she was still on the outs in school. Nobody was talking to her. Before line-up in the morning, cliques walled up firmly when she passed by. So much so that in defence, recent mornings, weather permitting, she had timed her arrival minute-close to roll-call. Recess-times, she hid out in a classroom, or the chapel, or a locked toilet stall. It was in there she overheard rotten-teeth Jainee poisoning the air with gossip: "No, no, no, it was when he first come. Last year, I think. Remember when Miss Lachu left to make baby? Well, it was then. Just after he come. Some standard-seven boys see them up the river, by Blue Basin pool."

"What they was doing?"

"Well, it wasn't holding hands."

"Well, what? What they was doing?"

"You know what they was doing." Jainee sounded out her simper.

"No. What? Tell me."

"They was in the soft sand by the river's edge, laying down. Together. He on top."

"No! Big Mr. Roland with skin-and-bones Natia Dassen! I don't believe you."

"Well, you don't have to. But I don't trust she. That whole family so. They over-hot. Look at she brother Preddy. You know 'bout he, right?"

"Yuh mean how he get Keah expel? Yeah, he's a bad one."

"No, no—it have more. . . . Oh! There's the bell. I have to meet with Sister Junia. We go talk later."

After the newsmongers left, for a safe minute or two Uxann remained locked in, her head buzzing with anxiety and frustration about the latest gossip's details. Was it what she knew . . . about Keah, about Paps? For the rest of the day she felt caged as a target at her front-desk seat. There was burn from every gleaming eye behind her. The titter from each whispered jibe aimed its rasp at her. Only twice she weakened her control and glanced back. There was no doubt. Each check, each face seemed mean and slinky.

She gave in at afternoon recess, lamely lied she was sick, and, maybe since it was Friday, Sister Marianne let her go.

▼▼▼

THE OUTSIDE WORLD remained all threat and censure even on her shortcut through the woods as she went straight home. From the garden fence she saw the top half of the kitchen door yawning wide. It seemed early for Keah, but with the present circumstances, who knew? So she unlatched the bottom half with extra clack and, as she entered, called loudly, "Ah home."

"That you, Girl Chile? Come here. Make a list. Ah going to the shop." It was Paps sitting at the dining-room table, grinning payday hearty, and not in the least drunk.

She took him in, muffling her surprise to listen, smell, sense the house for company. But she could find none.

Close to his chair she relaxed, leaning back on the table's edge. "How you home so early, Paps?"

Sideways, shrewdly, he looked at her. "Is only that surprising you?" he asked, grin hitching a down-mouthed slyness.

And right away she knew it was about his pride at keeping sober. Thinking of it, for the past two, three weeks, without her focusing and identifying it, he had been straight. Now what she had missed struck so hard, she couldn't face it. Instead, she said, "Well, at least we could just plain talk again."

Paps had heard her unsaid support, though. "Well, that couldn't be better," he said. "Ah figure we was ready for some changes 'round here. Big ones."

Uxann started, looked at him sharply. "Yuh mean Keah not . . ."

Paps held her eye unsteadily. "Nah . . . today she just off. But dat and other things go change. And all for de better."

Uxann looked away, mixing relief and disappoint-ment. Braving, she grasped his shoulder and, as it stiff-ened and flinched, said, "Hope so, Paps. I surely hope so."

He rose abruptly and turned for his room. "And lis-ten, midday tomorrow, we going hunting balata."

"Paps!" she screamed. "Oh, Paps! What a treat. You not making joke, huh?"

"Nah, Girl Chile. I serious like hot sun. And don't forget, hurry wit de shopping list." He went.

▼▼▼

BESIDES THE DEW, it was a damp Saturday dawn mainly from early drizzles. Uxann had followed their every spluttering start, anxiety about a wet day only fleeing when they altogether quit. Still, she couldn't relax, the balata hunt strong coffee to her spirits. So silver-grey foreday morning, she was up like a spark and tending the animals, happy to expend her energy in the soft light.

Afterwards, it was the outside kitchen fire and breakfast. She had hers, and for Paps left a mug of chocolate warming in the fire ashes. Then she dusted the house furniture, washed some personal clothes, and swept the front yard. Slick with eager sweat, returning to the back, she found a listless Paps slurping his chocolate in the kitchen. Alarmed at his sluggishness, she said, "Paps! You hads better get alive if we going for balata."

He slid her slow, blank eyes. "Balata?" he said, as if it were a foreign word. "Balata?"

"Paps!!!" she squealed to a spur of disappointment.

Then, through her distress, she glimpsed the bright

mischief behind his pretending eyes, caught the twitch of a smile at his lying mouth. Enough to rescue her lynched excitement. Enough to cover up. "You didn't fool me at all, Paps," she said. "Because you wouldn't have on yuh high-top leather boots, all laced up and everything." Even though she noticed the boots only as she mentioned them.

▼▼▼

HIGH SUN MIDDAY they were on their way, Paps' cutlass pinging through the overhanging brush as he re-formed this special track he'd chosen. Safe distance behind his sweaty effort, stopping altogether when necessary, Uxann followed. Fully at peace about it, peering beyond his lead, to her there was no sign of a track. So, voice raised against the slack slash of steel through plant life, she asked, "Yu'sure this is the way, Paps?"

Pling! Pling! Pling! his cutlass made way some three feet more. Then he turned slowly and held her tight-tight with his eye. With a stiff forefinger, he slicked away sweat dripping from his forehead. "Yuh asking a question? Or yuh telling me something?" he said.

Wriggling in the knot, Uxann dropped her eyes. Two

feet from her, a fat, iridescent earthworm slid leisurely along the damp, mottled ground. A bit farther, angled on a thin, beheaded stem, green as its perch, a praying mantis, eyes aswivel, waited and measured. Uxann felt the focus of those eyes. Their waiting whip. Its sting.

She heaved a contrite breath, and looked up to say "Sorry," just as Paps let go and resumed swinging steel, making his trail.

▼▼▼

EASY GOING NOW, as Paps' track had finally shown up. His good moods had returned, the two he'd fired down certainly helping. ("Is a hunt," he excused. "Liquor smell does soothe the animals.") She understood the drinks as celebration, and didn't mind.

Stopping asudden, jabbing the air, he turned and burst out, "Girl Chile! If ah lie, ah die! But yuh not goin' believe yuh own mouth. Is balata in esteem, dis. High-class, serious, original balata. No way, nohow agriculture, is natural everything. Even to how monkey plant it when dey pass. Yes! Total natural, dis balata. Show de only way shit-stink turn sweet balata flavour. Is how them seedlings shoot out under one-hundred-percent macaque manure. . . ." Sounding the howler himself, his own laughter coughed off the nonsense, allowing his return to leader-of-the-way.

▼▼▼

FOR A WHILE of this smooth track, he had been expounding on balata, particularly this special treeload he had discovered. But, following a man's length behind him, with all the swish and rustle of their passage, Uxann had missed most of his happy chatter. Her mind was preoccupied searching for a word to better describe their outing. By her sense of it, *hunt* missed the essence, was even offensive.

Hunt hinted at unpleasantness. Distress lurked in its background. There was desperate movement and violence, maybe even pain. The thrill in *hunt* had shiver and cringe. It wasn't tasty, dried the mouth, had no sweet in its flavour as balata did. *Hunt* didn't fit or describe what was their trip.

Their quest was ripe balata, bronzed and gold, somewhere up front. Secluded, inviting, wanting discovery, balata waited, with no messenger but scent. And mankind was not always keen with that. Regular mankind, that is, excepting Paps. Paps was canny to animal ways—was always pointing out their values to her. So, she wondered, maybe Paps might have a scene of their outing from animal eyes. Maybe if she broached it right, he might come up with a snugger-fitting word for their trip.

Paps abruptly stopped tracking, and was slowly scanning the foliage above. As Uxann caught up to him, he put a finger to his nose and whispered, "Check the air."

Gaze mimicking his, up and around, Uxann sniffed. Then sniffed again, and again as grinning Paps appraised her. Then she, too, grinned. For faint in the air, she had caught the message—a funky animal stench. Visitors. A mix of mongoose and manicou and monkey scent, and others, weak for balata, all.

It came to her then, the word she sought. "Spoor, Paps!" she shouted. "Is a balata spoor we on!"

He started at the volume, but, still gleam-eyed grinning, he nodded. "On de nose, Girl Chile. On de nose. Not long and it'll be on de tongue, too."

▼▼▼

"KEEP YUH EYE open, one in front and one on the ground. Long-'n'-swallow can't taste balata, but he does slake he chops on dem dat do."

Paps was late on that alert, though. Since back when he was cutting through the underbrush, Uxann had been on tippy-toe and quick-eyed for s-n-a-k-e-s (a word never said in the bush—these longfellows' home). Many times the settling of a lopped-off frond had suggested slinking cool-sliders, lethal and swift, maybe attacking, prayerfully fleeing. Each time, on high already, her alertness had increased. It piggybacked another excitement separate from fear and anticipation—a thrill that rode on how this spoor was hers and Paps' alone. A current spun from the two of them at this. Four eyes, four feet, four hands, two pounding pulses, one team close on the spoor.

Like soft flannel, a thought warmed into Uxann. "She never did this, though!" It was irresistible as a sigh, or her smirk.

▼▼▼

THE TREE WASN'T the tallest. Past the first straight-pole fifteen or so feet, it swelled out plump like a parasol, parading bunches and bunches of honey-yellow balata. They offset the leaves to grungy green almond shapes, dull plates offering gold.

"From here it look clean, huh? What yuh say?"

Two feet behind him, standing where he'd just stood, Uxann peered up over Paps' shoulder, where he had just peered. As such a secondhand expert, she said, "Kinda dim up in there, but I don't see anybody."

All the while squinting into the canopy, Paps sat on the ground and took off his boots. One more long look, a toss of his head. "Well, one way to find out," he said, and approached the tree trunk, feet hobbled with a rope lassoed tight around both insteps.

"Careful, Paps," said Uxann, unable to stop herself.

"Yuh telling I?" Paps grinned, looking like a schoolboy at Dosaro's.

A little jump up the bole and he grasped the tree around. Then, like a frog leaping, lifted by soles and hands and hobbled heels, quick-quick he mounted the bare trunk and reached the first branch. He hauled himself up and sat in a crook. Untying his hobble, barely out of breath, he called down, "So far, so-so."

Throat clamped in suspense since his first foot up, Uxann managed to grunt, "Uh-huh!"

But in truth, he was all right, soon comfortably jumping through the branches like a khaki-clad macaque. Boldly leaping despite the slender branches, holding on regardless of their extreme sways and swings.

"Paps!" Uxann shouted. "Them branches really thin, yu'know."

"Balata does bend without breaking," he yelled

back, flinging himself at yet another branch. Confident enough, but showing off, too.

As if it wanted only bats and acrobats to eat it, balata set out its fruit to be earned, right at the tips of rope-thin branches, displaying to the sun like jewels on a crown. Yet Paps was up there risking his life, flipping about, reaching hands and scrambling toes to cling and gather in choice bunches. Some he put in a gunnysack hung from his neck; some—when she had readied her skirt as a basket—he dropped while, tense like a vise, she spotted and rushed and shifted and waited, and most times caught the glowing bunch. Although sometimes missed, which still wasn't waste. For while Paps climbed and relocated, she sucked the juicy, spilled flesh of these broken balatas. And it wasn't long before her lips were sticky from shell gum, and with the big, black-eyed seeds in her pocket, she could begin to see a beaded necklace.

Paps' sudden screech of terror shivered her will and yanked her gaze upward. A blurred form—Paps?—was streaking down through the spindled branches, swifter than falling, never-stop bawling. Limber like water, it slid down the trunk and was gone. Yes, it was Paps yelling, ". . . TTOOOOOOOO!!"

A Paps crouched low with a buzzing cloud close behind. A Paps scooting nimbly through the underbrush, fleeing as if for life. But a Paps, too, still preciously hugging his gunnysack of balata. All of which changed her sympathies. Frightened fleet as was his retreat, it became greatly funnier.

But postponing laughter, Uxann promptly scrunched down on the ground and remained very still. For she'd finally understood Paps' yell. "Tattoo!" as in jep tattoo, the touchiest, evilest, stubbornest wasps of the wildwoods. Blind in their vengeance, bother them and weep, for they would follow any offender anywhere until they dropped.

There were but two escapes: Do like monkey and run through bush for leaves to slap them down, or do like manicou and curl up as if dead.

With Paps close in front of the trouble he'd incited, monkey was the only way for him, but bystander Uxann knew she was safe playing manicou.

Slow minutes after, she eased up to a cautious listening stance. No special concentration of wrathful buzz about. So she watchfully set off the way Paps had fled.

Like buzzing splatters along the vague tunnel of broken underbrush his passage had formed, wasps whirred and struggled to free themselves from the leaves or flowers or stems on which they'd impaled their blind fury. They would now struggle until they pulled away from their innards and fell to the ground as ant food. Uxann eyed warily as she passed, not so much for their spent stings as for the stupidity of their scratching frenzy.

The trail ended at a sluggish flow more ditch than

stream. Uxann heard "Hhssstt! Hhssstt!" and had to search for a moment before seeing him breaking surface from a knee-deep pool like an over-toothed manatee, slime and muck sliding off his head. "Careful," he whispered through his grin, "dey might be still around. Resting on the branches"—snigger—"trying to draw a line on de ol' man." Another snigger as he drew his face back underwater.

He got off lucky, only three stings. One over the right eye, one on the back of his neck, one on his left wrist. He selected and crushed together three different bush leaves, then rubbed the potion on the swelling flesh. In a quick minute, the stingheads were showing, so that with her fingernails Uxann could pull the poison tips out.

After that, they returned to the tree and were silently collecting Uxann's heap of balata when a heavy rustling in the foliage made them look up. From the lowest branches of an adjacent tree, a big male macaque rouge had been quietly observing them. He was swinging on now. With a queer thrill, Uxann wondered, How long he there watching?

▼▼▼

LATE AFTERNOON, HOMEWARD bound, they were steadily
trudging along. Paps had been pensive most of the way.
Maybe it was jep tattoo poison, or the watching macaque, or maybe he was just tired from all his frisking
around.

To challenge his mood, Uxann caught up to him and
asked, "Paps, you wasn't 'fraid you'd hurt yourself
jumping around in the branches just now?"

"Lehme tell yuh, Girl Chile," he said, "yuh body not
a keepsake. Yuh have it for use. Harder de better, I
say."

He went quiet again for a muddy patch of track, while
Uxann, grinning privately, recalled his hard-used flight
from the jep tattoo.

Paps interrupted, "Yu'know, Girl Chile, long time
ago when rainbow had all the colours, matters between
animals and mankind was real nice. Back then, everybody used to get along fine, visit and discuss, have
games together, and so on. Never a word in anger,
never a spiteful act. No cruelty at all . . ."

He walked without speaking for several paces, while

Uxann practiced patience. She knew his way of story-telling. Interrupt now, and she risked losing the rest. So she kept apace and waited.

"Yep," he started again, "it used to be real nice. More harmony than green. Then mankind discover work and profit, and all asudden, when a man was weak, he had to work for a man who was stronger, or die one way or de other. And because a man was weak enough, he'd work for only spit-out. Of course, Strongman call dat system profit. Weak man call it slavery.

"Meanwhile, monkey looking on and figuring. To him it look like Strongman soon will need more labour. And whatever yuh say about monkey, more than able and agile, he lazy like mud. All he know 'bout work is it don't die. So he decide to separate with mankind ways. So, from dat day forward, he went silent in de presence of man—no words at all, just stop like dumb. Save himself from slavery, he did. Couldn't talk, so couldn't take de dreadman orders."

A meditative grunt, and Paps went silent, leaving the swish of their passage dominant. A whisper that set her mind considering his fable. Firmly on monkey's side, she nevertheless could sympathize with the seduction of slavery. She only had to think of her and Keah these days. Just twice a week she came now, for which Uxann was content, since it was usually to wash heavy clothes and sweep the big, gravelly front yard.

Uxann saw nothing more awkward and unbecoming than washing clothes on a scrub board in a tub. All that jerking up and down, up and down, bent from the waist, arms pumping from the shoulders, snapping up and down, up and down, wrestling with wet heavy clothes, slurping cloth with grungy froth flying everywhere, on your nose, in your eyes, while you looked like some fat, funny puppet on a jerk-string. Keah, on her part, seemed to enjoy the splash and lash of the water, laughed with every dousing, never minded being wet.

Same way with the yard-cleaning. Each time she swept the front yard, Uxann contended with a private nightmare. She'd be sweeping, bending over to push the handful of cocoyea broom and the pile of fallen leaves before it, and there would come a gust, one of those whirly wind demons. And it would rush right under her skirts and puff them up over her face, and expose for everyone's amusement her big bloomers and oversized thighs, while she tried to disappear or die in a steamy haze of embarrassment.

And Keah? Wind up her skirts? It'd only merry her!

Yes, monkey had a point. Full-time slavery was no good. But maybe just a little bit of it Uxann could excuse, like a servant off and on, to do hated chores. Like a Keah. Although with Keah it was more than plain slavey. She was still sort of a friend. For despite

everything, Uxann still looked forward to her company, her cheeriness, her devil-may-care, her gossip—
which wasn't school stuff anymore. These days she
trafficked adult business—weighty matters with subtle
levels of intrigue and complexity, insides that astonished and sometimes kept Uxann up mulling late nights.
This Keah, helper and friend, Uxann continued to welcome, and two days a week she figured to ignore the
after-dinner goings-on.

▼▼▼

BRIGHT AND EARLY Monday morning, Uxann was up and
busy at her chores. For although she had studied until late
last night, she was making time for some last-minute
cramming. Term tests for promotion began today, and
she intended to do well. The schedule was math in the
morning, nature study after lunch, then school was dismissed. So she worked swiftly, rehearsing various math-
ematical formulae she had committed to memory,
growing in confidence with each successful recollection.

Since the sisters were always advising a hearty breakfast before examinations, on the outside fire she brewed
some thick chocolate intended to wash down a solid

piece of dasheen left over from Sunday's supper. She left the meal warming by the fireside and, to make better time, decided to shower and change into her uniform before eating.

While dressing, she heard Paps thump by en route to his morning rendezvous with the banana stool. From her room, she yelled, "Morning, Paps."

A gruff "Morning, Girl Chile" returned with the bang of the bottom half of the kitchen door closing. Then, ready with her school bag, she went to eat.

First bite of the dasheen, her belly went squeamish as if the food were spoiled. She sniffed the dasheen to make certain—it wasn't—then nibbled from another part, and swallowed. Reluctantly, her stomach accepted the morsel. So much so that she decided to pass on the solid food and settle for the warm chocolate, her favourite drink. As she sipped it, though, a sudden, steamy nausea rose up through her and made her feel faint. Sweaty, almost swooning, her innards slack, she dropped into a chair and breathed deeply through her open mouth, waiting for the dizzy to pass. When it was slow to, misreading her slack bowels, she tottered to the toilet and sat and pushed and strained and waited for something to happen. But nothing did, except the faintness faded some, and the flush of sweat cooled down. She got up and washed her face and, still discomforted, went for her school bag.

Paps was in the kitchen brewing his coffee. One look at her and he said, "Yuh looking like yuh swallow yuh liver. Yuh awright?"

"Was until I tried to eat just now."

"Is that stale food yuh like that cramping yuh stomach. A lick of lime or some salt on yuh tongue will cut the upset."

Which it did when she took a pinch. "Thanks, Paps," she said, then left for school.

▼▼▼

THE MATH, AS usual, was a breeze. With still half an hour to go, Uxann had finished the problems and was re-checking, although confident she had well managed them. A few more minutes for courtesy, then she handed in her answers and left the room, conscious of envious and other eyes on her. Outside, the schoolyard was empty, everyone else in regular classes or taking exams. Though it was still some time before lunch-bell, she felt peckish. So she found an out-of-the-way spot by the school garden to eat the mango john her ongoing diet permitted. Two bites and a swallow into it, she gagged and, with both hands pressed against the toolshed, leaned over and threw up mainly strings of elastic slime and the half-chewed morsel of yellow mango meat, sickening herself moreover from the smell of the vomit and the forceful spasms of her rejecting stomach.

Anxiously searching about, she wiped her mouth and watering eyes, thankful that no one had seen. Then quick to the toilets, she washed the sourness from her mouth, although not from her system. Just in time, too, for when she returned to the schoolyard, Eralee was there, second finished with the math test, and full of admiring questions: "But, Uxann, how you always done so quick, girl? You find it was easy?"

Stomach roiling queasy, but face composed, Uxann said, "Except for the train problem, it wasn't so hard."

"What you get for that one?" asked Eralee.

"Which part of it? Already I can hardly remember," Uxann countered, skeptical of her sudden examination-day popularity, and unwilling to tell answers to her competition in math. Then she was saved as three or four girls came up to make general discussion of the exam.

Uxann didn't take much part. Still not feeling right, she was trying to switch her mind to nature-study matters, while managing the contradiction of her guts: Hungry as she was, she couldn't stomach even the slightest thought of food. What she wished for was a lick of salt, or lime.

But soon the bell rang, and it was back into the class-room for the afternoon test. Which commanded full attention from her queasy stomach, as she managed quite to her satisfaction.

▼▼▼

THE LAST DAYS before long vacation, school was letting out after lunchtime recess. With the extra free time, Dosaro's became a primary destination for those who knew a way in. Governor plums and sugar apples were riping. But because Mr. Stingy was aware of the end-of-term schedule, the venture bore more than usual risk. In the morning schoolyard, along with brags of raiding some exceptional fruit, there were also admissions of several skin-of-the-teeth escapes. Playing spoiler with bull-pistle in hand, Dosaro seemed to have planted him-self in the arbour. Uxann listened to the excited re-countings without many qualms. Although normally she drooled over the fat plums and sweet, crumbly meat of the crusty sugar apples, these days it was less-sweet fruit she craved, like the sour-sweet pomme-rac, which grew a good safe distance away from the main attrac-tion.

So Wednesday afternoon, after the jostle at the school

gate, she dawdled behind the other village girls until it was safe to slip away and use her private gate into the arbour. Once inside, cautious but directly, she headed for the pomme-rac. Under the shade of the fruit trees, she prowled swiftly along, imagining she was a big hunting cat on the spoor—a great ocelot, or a stalking jaguar—a dangerous creature exaggerating at alertness, pausing frequently to listen as she went, well seeing not to be seen.

Her raid went easy as kissing hands. As expected, she had her target all to herself and, after making mongoose-certain from behind an old immortelle tree, she collected her choice of rosy, sour-sweet fruit. Conscious of her drooling, but helpless, she stuffed down the first half dozen to cut the edge of her craving. Then, thinking of the morrow, she made more deliberate selection from fallen fruit, and filled her bag. Afterwards, sated and well stocked, but still sampling the occasional, she set her footsteps to a leisurely way home.

Her heading was a bamboo stool where a creek entered Dosaro's property. Although the stave fence spanned the ten-feet-wide stream, the water was clear and but thigh-deep, and it was nothing to wade nearer the raised bamboo clump, duck under the fence, and exit the watchman's domain not far from the public roadway. To avoid the evidence of her wet passage, she intended to take off her skirt and sneakers at the creek's edge, then re-dress outside.

Just within sight of the bamboo patch, anticipating the cool of the creek and wanting to lessen the shock to her feet, Uxann stopped and doffed her sneakers. She tied them by their strings and hung them around her neck, shrugging at the immediate spot of mud sloughed off onto the left pocket of her bodice. The extra bit of washing would've well had its worth in pomme-rac. As she rose to continue, she heard the snigger.

Female and full of nervous excitement it was—and something other that Uxann couldn't bring to mind. She instantly crouched back down, slinking into the underbrush for concealment. Heartbeat pounding a hasty minute, she waited tensely for whoever it was to pass. But she heard no approach, the person seeming to have stayed where she was—somewhere just ahead. Or maybe she had gone on down the creek. A minute more Uxann waited, then decided to venture on and get out of the arbour. So, still in semicrouch, with eyes keened and ears straining, she crept towards the bamboo stool.

She was close to the water—its gurgling perhaps thirty feet away—when she heard the gruff, demanding male voice. And in response, the low moan of the female that began as a "Noooo" and continued slow and long to a sigh of support and surrender. Then Uxann could halfway see them through the curtain of fat and slender bamboo shoots, the man pulling the woman into the heart of the bamboo clump, lifting her legs up and over splayed shafts, handling her firmly, pulling certainly, helping her in. And the woman, slack-limbed, compliant, her eyes fixed to his face as if tethered to something there. As if he were a macawoeul and she a chicken hypnotized and ready to be consumed, but uncaring of the peril, even courting it. Then the man had her one-armed about the waist, roughly clamping her to him, while he pulled at her skirt, at her breasts, baring them, then bending his head down in a serpent's bite. And the woman with hands busy at his pants, head thrown back offering her neck, her breasts, her self, as if abandoned to his desire and taking pleasure from it. Then they sank to the ground, embraced in their eager struggle, their bamboo-leaf pallet rustling like gravel, a background rattle to the grunts and moans of their out-of-sight coupling.

Tense and thrilled to goose bumps, Uxann was returned to herself then, and, alert once more, slipped out of the arbour.

▼▼▼

THE SIGHT OF them was seared into her mind—the woman's harnessed gaze, the man's strong hands, rough and certain, managing her—bits of their scene recurring in haphazard sequence as she walked the public road, each image renewing the thrills, expanding a strange tension that seemed to focus at her fancy. Tightening her butt muscles as she walked, although partly relieving, also demanded further forceful squeezing up her thighs, heightening the current stirring within her.

Flushed and breathless it made her, and all asudden, she couldn't bear the open, crunchy, graveled road. So, quickly estimating her location, she jumped the storm drain and pushed into the high woods to make a private pathway to her usual shortcut home. But it was no better there. Among the quiet hum of forest sounds, memory's invasion sameway came: the woman's drawn-out sigh, her neck thrown back submitting with a moan; the man's clasping arm, his pose untender, cocksure of compliance. The thought of such surrender, the mystery of it, triggered a sluggish flow that melted her marrow, making her weak, so that she had to stop and lean against a gnarled and knobby tree trunk, holding painful strong to it, embracing the bark's hardness, pressing as if for entry, as a charge of extreme pleasure made slurry of her blood, concentrating deliciously at her crotch, creeping warmer and warmer through every channel within her, threatening a swoon.

Then a flash of happening unfurled untidily in tangled swirl. A moment of silver—a pocket of brilliance, her mind peaceful, her body atingle all over.

Insights knotted, fragments cross-matching, flooding her. Was this the nectar Keah sought, sip by sip, by sip? A slippery at her fancy she knew without recognizing, and so sweet! with a splash of guiltiness to this feeling, too; a torture tempting, even as she shifted clothes and lipped a curled finger to the swamp, then slipped it up and tongued the tangy soak she sharply breathed in, as came a subtle fear this fire would pounce again, destroying her like now, as hope it would, and take command, as suddenly she knew a common female sharing with, maybe, even Keah?

It was all too much to bear. This too-swift descending drum-bolt throbbing compulsion from her fancy. A newly ruling realm that must diminish her.

Although it didn't, when it was done, and calmly gone, except for a dread that its power would return, or wouldn't.

▼▼▼

SINCE DISCOVERY DAY and two religious holidays were falling right at the end of long vacation this year, they upped it a week to seven. Another unit to the sentence! was how Uxann saw the extra. By the second Monday home, she was sorely missing the routines of getting up and going to school, of study, the companionship of the road. Or maybe just the road, for it wasn't for people she pined. It became her mood to brood the days away lazing around in her room, or gazing from the outside kitchen window, or sitting in the funky animal pens.

Two setting ducks had hatched their eggs, producing thirty or so fluffy yellow ducklings. Following their mothers about the yard in scrounging for food allowed Mr. Mongoose to be eating well of strays. The clutches were down to but twenty-two now. Paps wasn't at all pleased. With the vacation begun and Uxann home, the project was to build and fence in a pond for the ducklings. Idle Uxann would maintain it, wouldn't she? Uxann shrugged and agreed, "Sure, Paps."

To best use the lie of the land, he had decided on the far backyard corner beyond the animal pens. Sunday, Paps had some cronies over to form and fence around the pond, and slope a channel into it from the standpipe.

Part of Uxann's later-on job was to populate the pond with millionfish and coscarobs and other canal life. But now, while the men created a heavy sand-and-concrete bottom for the eight-by-ten pond, her major task was cooking up a pelau to tantalize their mid-afternoon break.

She had Paps slaughter the pushy, overgrown drake while she picked fresh pigeon peas from the garden. The pain and suffering done, she feathered and seared and gutted and cleaned the hefty bird before cutting it up into hungry-man chunks. Then was the initial browning down and stewing with coconut milk, in preparation for the busted peas, then the rice. In control in her element, happy time passed swiftly, and by twoish the kitchen was sending off such enticing aromas that the men were making too-frequent pass-bys under any pretext whatsoever.

So straightforward, foreman Paps declared breaktime, and allowed the men to sit and sample her sweet-cooking hand. As much appetite as rare delight had them sucking bones and licking fingers of the food, with sighs and praises, the sole complaint being insufficient second rounds. It was only with much badgering and bribes promising rum that Paps got them to return and complete the job.

▼▼▼

WITH PETITE CAREEM, for a couple of days the weather was nice enough to let Uxann try a few trips to nearby creeks and canals to fish and fulfill her promise in the bargain. But she was feeling off and distracted, and although there was success, her effort remained half-hearted. The feeling fact was, she was awaiting Keah's company, who didn't come around until midday Thursday, having heard of the project and perking with enthusiasm over it.

Then she was there high spirits and all, and in two twos, equipped with pails and makeshift nets, they were off to the woods to kidnap pond-life.

Wasn't too long, either, before the gossip began to flow: "Yuh hear about Eralee and dem?" Keah's eyes flared like a flambeau to the cesspit.

"No. Tell me."

"Well, they have it to say dat she and she li'l brother have another father."

"No! Who say?"

"I can't tell yuh dat."

"Why not? Yuh know I won't be telling nobody."

"Ah just can't tell yuh," insisted Keah.

Uxann pouted. "Yuh don't trust me."

Keah stopped walking and held her eye. "Don't try dat on me, Uxann. Yuh know is not so. If ah could ah would. But ah can't."

"Why yuh can't, then?" asked Uxann crossly.

"Is a cut-mih-tongue promise dat ah make," Keah said solemnly, her eyes glistening.

An odd feeling of guilt hit Uxann, and she looked away, convinced. Silently they walked on again, an awkwardness in the air, the sharp point of the gossip dulled.

Keah took Uxann's hand and stopped them. "Uxann, don't feel bad. Is the same ah would do for yuh, yu'know. Ah like talk, is true. But ah could hold a promise like a vise, too."

She said it so sincerely, Uxann didn't mind anymore. True as her smile, she said, "Is okay, in truth. It don't make a difference who tell yuh. Just tell me."

"Now we talking!" said Keah, eyes again a shining beam on intimate mischiefs. "Well, if yuh really don't mind, lehme finish the scores."

From then, for the rest of the outing, the village's who-was-whose-and-who-wasn't business flew.

In between, they also collected—from tadpoles to water spiders—two good pails full of pond-life.

▼▼▼

SHE HAD BEEN putting it off, convincing herself that the weight was only in her mind. Then, Saturday mid-morning, she and Paps composing the shopping list, she pleading pork—hog maws, pigfeet, and such—the intention, souse. "Paps! How long since yuh so don't like souse? Eh? And think that Christmas coming. This would come like practice. What yuh say, huh? Please!!!"

But Paps wasn't playing. His cold eye squeezed her, embarrassed, out of her play-plaintive voice. "Well, yuh used to like the souse I make like dog on marrow-bone," she concluded sulkily, and penciled hard lines through the "Souse" entry of the list before her.

Silence swelled like seas, distancing them.

Paps reached out a line. "Is not my tastes I thinking about. Maybe we should shorten dis food list some."

And from his tone alone, Uxann divined the fault. Automatic denial hooked in her craw and ground like grit as he went on, "Take a look at yuhself, Girl Chile. Mirror don't lie. Yuh swelling up buffo-buffo like bullfrog in trouble. Ah mean, yuh have to take a look at yuhself!"

She heard his every word. But what printed in her mind was his bullfrog picture—its glistening eyes abulge with stupid gulping, blowing up its neck to a ridiculous windbag trying to frighten. Which image breached an understanding, solid and unmentionable between them—a compact that he would never so harshly show her up.

She left him to his listings. One look that threw a dagger, then escape to her room to stomach his betrayal. And regarding the shopping list? As far as she was concerned, he didn't need to shop at all. From now on it would be hard ever to eat his food again.

▼▼▼

SHE ACTIVELY CUT down, served herself smaller portions, then tossed half of every plate to the hogs. She also totally abandoned after-dinner specials. Yet, especially in her breasts, she continued to grow, as did her sudden cravings for sour fruit, like chenettes dipped in lemon-juice, and pommes cyteres in pepper sauce, and green cherries and mangoes, the more tongue-tying the better. Those out of season, or just unavailable, she pined for while drooling from the dreams.

With Keah's every visit she remained on the brink of broaching the quandary, only deep shame at her constant enlargement forestalling her leap. Then, after lunch on Friday, Uxann was gazing at the garden through the outside kitchen window. And though she wasn't due, who but Keah should burst, bangles clanging, screaming through the door space, "Uxann! Uxann! Yuh get a distinction! Yuh beat everybody flat!"

The startle from Keah's entry was swift away as elation of her news exploded Uxann's spirits skywards, although collected, and sailing smooth and graceful, and . . .

"Don't just goggle at me, girl. If ah lie, ah die. Dey post results dis morning. Yuh beat back everybody. And plus dat with distinction in math."

From her clouds on high, Uxann floated to the pitcher, and poured the small calabash half-full, and sipped the soft rainwater contentedly. Just to show that she could speak, she said, "I was kinda sure about the maths . . ."

"Seyeh definitely have to keep yuh in school now. De nuns go make him."

Puzzled at her train of thought, Uxann said, "He was going to anyhow."

Keah shrugged. "Whatever. But now he got to."

As it occurred to her, Uxann, intense, said, "Let *me* tell Paps, okay?"

"Sure," Keah returned with a shrewd eye, "is your results."

More to break the pause developing, Uxann asked, "Who come second?"

"Eralee. And she get a distinction in nature study. Ah don't think she know yet, though. De family working a dasheen plot up de hills."

From Uxann's heights, it was more good news for all, she being easy with Eralee's success since it had stayed out of her pet subjects.

". . . eh? How come yuh let she beat yuh in nature study?" Keah was repeating.

Uxann looked at her, blank for an answer.

"I mean," Keah went on, "she okay. But is yuh everybody was expecting from. Yuh is de most studious, and everything."

"But Eralee does study, too. And she smart."

"She work hard at it," Keah admitted. "But she not a natural. Everybody know when yuh fat, books come easier—" She caught herself and ended, "Well, yuh know . . ."

Uxann started for the pitcher, then realized there was still water in her calabash. She sipped demurely, and tossed the rest out the window. It formed a crystal lace falling to the ground, as a momentary rainbow glittered and was gone with the splatter.

Keah left soon after.

▼▼▼

IT WAS THE last time Keah came. Next two, then three weeks, every Thursday morning Paps took away the dirty heavy clothes. Friday evening he returned them clean-smelling of mothballs and neatly folded.

On the second Friday, during supper, watching grim Paps devouring cassava dumplings as if they'd insulted him, Uxann broached the disappearance. "How they going down?" she asked to loosen him up.

Paps finished chewing a dumpling away, then raised a grave eye to her and nodded reluctantly. "They not doing so bad." Then he returned to his wars.

She felt like crouching in the middle of her worry web, but still she let a strand reach out. "Paps, yu'notice Keah didn't come this week . . ."

Right away, with not even an upward glance, his brusque grunt chopped down the probe. "Mmhnn-hmmnn!"

Uxann knew it well to leave the matter bleeding.

THE HOUSE BECAME a cage as Paps closed off himself from her. And Uxann racked and worried her mind every pace of the maze in that cage. Whole days she spent just searching for whys, and all tracks returned to her size. (*F-a-t* being the one unutterable word.) When she couldn't stand the blank quiet of the house anymore, and if it was a time with folks less likely about, she would sneak into the open yard. Although sometimes the brightness was too much, so she'd hide in the shade of the zebus' empty pen. Or, if the weather was gloomier, she'd sit on an old box by the duck pond and watch the new families' antics.

Seldom these looked new anymore. Fluffy, yellow puffballs were more often squeaky, shivering mudslicks searching for a spot under Mama Duck's warm wing. But off and on, spic and span, both clutches would take to foraging the pond, all twenty of them, sharp-eyed beaks bobbing in formation, slipping along graceful and light on the water like stately golden leaves on air. The sight of the ducklings was all that could yeast her daydreams these days. They, too, were growing ungainly every day.

▼▼▼

SHE WAS THERE at the pond on payday Friday, comparing, when Paps came off the field track on his way to the backyard gate. One glance and she knew he had been drinking. The grumble in the story he mumbled to himself added that there were no good moods to it. He hadn't noticed her, and to keep it so, Uxann quietly drew herself up against the fence-post and let him pass. It was months he had stopped drinking. What calamity had broken him back to this mulling in rum bottles? It was only these last few weeks that he had changed. And from a cruel part of her mind the logic followed through: *Was only since her weight went out of control that Paps lost spirits.*

She remained in the yard as long as the tension let her leave him the house. To busy the time, she set to shifting and fluffing out the bag of a cotton dress she had taken to wearing. It was cool and especially loose, and hardly touched her prickly skin. Even its faded dun-brown shade was growing on her. It tinged of passive sympathy.

"Uxann!" Paps' voice came strong and clear. No sign of booze at all. The trouble was he called her by name. But, her manner composed, she went straightaway to her fate.

He was in the dining room standing next to his chair by the table. His flat glass halved, the bottle of bush rum three-quarters full and open where his plate would've been. The liquor's surface trembled like thick oil in wind, its clove molasses flavour floated to her nose. Although she couldn't stay with the smell because of the manner in his eyes—the way they seemed a smoldering coal-pile built of rage and shame and even logs of hatred.

Distraction was a gurgly rattle that freed her eyes to search out, just as he did, too. The glass and bottle clicked against each other from his fingers drumming the table's edge. He took up the glass and gulped down a mouthful. When he looked back at her, his eyes were only sad. He said, "Girl Chile, why yuh don't sit down and let we talk dis thing out?"

She said, "Yes, Paps," and sat primly straight-backed in her chair.

He sat and eyed her, and slowly shook his head, then turned away and sipped from his glass, as if to help support his sight. He looked her over again, from head down to feet, leaving his gaze on the floorboards, then heaved his sadness to his chest and started. "I always try mih best for you. You know dat, Uxann. I know you know it. I do mih best for Girl Chile. Mih house is mine, and fine. I do dat for Girl Chile. I is de man to talk to for a favour in dis place. I be dat man for Girl Chile. I never want. Mih house never want. Mih table always feed you. I thought you learn mih better ways. And I always forget mih bad ones. You musta learn dem too. And schupid me, I bring de book to you. . . ."

Uxann was scrambling through his words for a meaning, some clue towards which she could launch a defence, when she caught the bit about books and learning, and memory struck a spark of hope into her mind. It probably had to do with the exam results!

With all her worries these last weeks, she had clean forgotten to tell him the news. He seemed over-hurting about it, but maybe that was the liquor at work, talking its mind through him. She attended more sharply then, waiting for a gap in his line of thought that she could jump through.

". . . and man can't fathom woman. Each one have dey way. So I as man can take getting fool. Is Life itself dat fool we. We always expecting better. But Life don't make no promise. Is only we. Goat don't make sheep. Fruit fall but!"—he snapped his fingers—"far from de tree. Life is a roll in a barrel. No matter how you climb, it coming back and catching you. And is but one clear way out. . . ."

Paps seemed to be aiming for Talparo and shooting at the fullmoon, as he would describe it, just as, mid-thought, her spot came. Set to spring her news, Uxann caught a pause as she saw the tear form and roll slowly out his right eye, and race down the edge of his nose, and teeter there as if gathering courage for the rest of the trip. Then she couldn't help but weep. As company.

The first she could quiet her sniffles, she blurted, "Paps, I come out first in the exam and get distinction in maths," then succumbed to tears again.

He had stood up, and was staring down at her, a furious frown on his face. But he was puzzled, too. His hands strangling the air right in front of her face, he said, "What is going on with you, Girl Chile? Yuh going to talk to me serious, or what?"

"I just did forget to tell you, Paps. I was worried about . . ."

"Worried about what?" Paps coached. "Eh? Worried about . . . ?"

"Getting fat, Paps!" she shouted, outraged at her own rudeness, but compelled to repeat it as loudly. "FAT, Paps. I'M FAT!"

Paps sat down as if plucked by the air, an odd look on his face. He reached for the glass and drained it, halved it again from the bottle, and left it there. He clasped his hands between his knees, looked her in the eye, and said, "So you want to tell me, or you want me to ask?"

"I don't know what to tell you, Paps. I can't understand. I just getting fatter all the time. Whatever I do. Whatever I eat. It don't make a difference. . . ." She couldn't go on for the snot in her throat.

Paps reached over face-to-face, and gripped her shoulders with hands that surprised, they so big and strong. Pinching her slightly, the fresh rum breath like vapour from his mouth, he asked, "Uxann, yuh know why yuh getting fat so?"

It wasn't a question. His manner was alive with firm knowledge. He would tell her, now! She locked expecting eyes on his.

"Girl Chile! Uxann!" he said. "Yuh making baby!"

Slip-sliding silly, as if on mud in her mind, the words struggled to pass on the idea. Only their outrageousness came through. Then the laughter, mobbing, unstoppable. It overthrew in gales, in gusts of helpless glee. It swept her from the chair like she was empty cloth, and thrashed her on the floor. She smacked at the boards till her palms stung, and still she could not stop. Looking up for mercy, she saw Paps' face break soft and very handsome in an odd grin. Then he reached to help her up, and the crazy mirth sneaked out of the way for her true, mightier joy.

She kept hold, hugging his arm tight, felt her face against the shoulder button of his khaki coverall. She felt able to be light again, and said into his shoulder, "Paps, how I could be making baby? None of the boys does even look at me."

He stiffened immediately. Into it came a quiver. He shoved her roughly away, stumbling her past the chair. Furious, he glowered at her, staggering in place not to approach, as if barely maintaining some personal boundary. "Ah was willing to hear you, but yuh still trying to deny it," he raged. "For what? Eh? To make me out yuh personal fool? Like mother like chile! Huh? Well, not so! God blast you to Hell with yuh kind! And don't let me put mih eyes on you again!"

And with a look of angry disgust on his face, he turned and stomped out of the room.

Driven by his conviction, she reached hands to her belly, and pressed and kneaded and tried to assess objectively. She had felt pregnant animals before. And although it was impossible, she had to admit to a hard breadfruit body in there that did support him.

▼▼▼

HER BODY WAS stretched tight. Her mind was stretched tight. The world was stretched tight about her at the strangeness of the situation. How? How? Her mind tried to weigh the monstrous puzzle, hard as the lump in her belly. How? How? She tried to approach the mountain of it. Try as she might, she couldn't figure a way though self-banished to her room all barren night. Without balm of sleep, she sought for supernatural reasons, and quivered at recollecting the Gabilan. But that was Anancy story. Uxann was real life, she argued, as over and over she stroked the tight mound of the puzzle. One main point she stood on. She had never done it with a man! Had never done it at all. Except for that time in the woods after spying on the couple. But that wasn't the same. Of this she made certain, checked every reference in the index of her nature-study textbook. And every one suggested that, upwards from protozoa, there had to be a male. And though she might be fat, she surely wasn't bacteria. And there wasn't even a male she could imagine who would have.

The frustration threading her confusion was that Keah didn't come around anymore. Was it so, then she could at least anticipate some future clearing-up. Ten thousand times that night, her hands unconsciously sought the hard lump in her belly.

Impossible? But once when she was quiet at it, she thrilled to a maybe pulse.

▼▼▼

SHE MUST HAVE dozed off. For sun in the clouds, mid-morning was bright when she woke. The house, on a careful listen, was empty quiet. Then, in the bathroom mirror, the whole bacchanal washed back into her mind, thrilling, depressing, bewildering, unyielding, vast. How could she be . . . ? Her mind refused.

She stripped and looked her body over. Forget the breasts! From gentle grades, they were now plump ranges on her chest, but down past them, her belly didn't bunch out that much. Only when she looked at it expecting something it did. But in fact, if she looked at herself uncritically, she didn't look babying at all.

Perked by the moment's relief, she did her toilette, threw on her big dress, and tiptoed into the house.

In the middle of the dining table, a copybook page was held down by the rum bottle. There was writing on it. Uxann picked it up and read:

U haav no odder bed n bord, so till dis ting torne dis wae aw dat, u kan stae.

Onli dat u muss nt let yorself b ceen owtcyd d hows nn daelyt n e moor.

An n e ting u hav to sae, u muss ryte it down. I wull reed eet well.

N u muss stae owt my syte.   SEYEH.

As Uxann cyphered it through, sniffling, her hands made that newfound wonder trip to her belly.

▼▼▼

HE HAD BARRED up the cage of the house with heavy brown-cotton curtains, each with the same ugly, dark-green vine pattern swirling up like bars, over every window with a face to the world. The front rooms were curtained. The little window in the toilet was. Even her own room! For he could move like a cat when he wanted to. A whole forest of vines screened light from entering the inside kitchen. And a dispirited head poked through the in-between space confirmed that the broad, never-close wooden flap-windows around the outside kitchen—all four were pulled down and latched.

There was a large calabash of milk on the counter of the outside kitchen. Uxann sniffed it and took a sip, deciding zebu from the thick cream and strong smell. She used her finger to stir the cream back in some, then licked the finger clean, and washed it down with a long gulp. Every pleasure about fresh milk remained perfect.

But when did he milk them? she wondered. And manage the other animals, too. As she was certain they were all—from ducklings to hogs—taken care of. And then the windows. He must've woken early to sweat at all this. It must have been Shame and Rage driving him that hard. To go through threading those ugly curtains, then hanging them, his eyes dread as he soft-footed past, watching her sleep. Oh, how he must have hated her!

Hands caught to her belly, the fingers kneaded and searched the basic puzzle. How?

▼▼▼

FOR BREAKFAST, SHE mashed up a slice of zaboca in a
pocket of roast-bake, and washed it down with some
milk. She rinsed knife and saucer and cup in the inside-
kitchen sink, then replaced them to shelves and drawers.
Then she needed the toilet—these days her bladder
seeming a strainer. Brushed her teeth once more. Studied every grimace as she worked. Then, pressing and
pulling close her dress this way and that, she used up the
mirror with a critical eye for a long while.

Later on, Uxann ate again, and did her teeth again,
and watched the mirror some more, until the toilet was
important. Then she took a nap.

▼▼▼

SHE WOKE TO the clump of his boots into the shoe
box in the outside kitchen: an idea of hers to catch dirt
before it entered the house. Feeling the need, she got out

of bed and started for the door to the toilet. Mid-stride, though, she stopped and, treading softly, went instead to the window and carefully cracked the curtain aside. To her surprise, it was close to night darkness out. At a loss for what to do, she went back to the bed and sat, and waited wistful for sounds of his presence. After a while she lay on her back, listening. That way, also, the whip in her bladder lost some of its sting.

He was cooking in the outside kitchen. There was the hot, hissy busy of something fry-stewing, then the hush as the pot-cover muffled it. For a bit, while Uxann didn't think of her bladder, quiet hid him again. She bet herself that by her count to fifty, she'd hear him stir the pot. At seventy-three, deciding she'd gone too quickly, she began again, and got to twenty-seven when, with a tremor, she heard a floorboard briefly creak outside her door as he passed. Then came the pot-cover clatter again.

She got up swiftly, was out the door and into the toilet. And not a moment too soon. Done, she didn't flush, but went to the door and, ear to the board, listened, long and double-checking. Then, sucking up courage, she zipped back to the door of her room. Safely catching her breath, an image from the toilet just left returned to her mind: Gathering cobwebs, turned down in the far corner from the shower, was a pink-flowered, enameled posie. The same one she'd used back in the old house, and exactly the need right now. It was a must to go back. Closing her eyes and cocking her head from side to side, she tried to locate him. Put her head to the door, then her ear to the floor. All quiet. Lay on her back in the bed and concentrated. Nothing. He was lost in his quiet again.

▼▼▼

WHEN SHE AWOKE again, she didn't have to go to the window. The quiet had that quivering rhythm of night. The crickets, the frogs keeping time. The off-and-on flutter from the fowl roost. The big critters' cries and calls from afar. The house soothing about her with sighs. Tiptoeing to the door, she opened to hear Seyeh softly snoring. So she was free.

First thing first. She took the posie into her room and gave it a test squat. The position hardly felt awkward at all, and although the pot was small compared to the toilet bowl, it was quite adequate.

That done, soft-walking heel and toe, she ventured into the shadowed house. There was a note on the dining table, pale in the dimness. Uxann picked it up, and went and cracked the curtain to read:

u kn lyt a no smok fyar nn d dae   Seyeh

In the kitchen, neatly stacked under the fireside, she saw a bundle of fresh-cut, well-dried firewood. In the fireside itself, he had left in the embers an enamel bowl of stewed-up corned beef spliced by a bundle of braised bodie beans. Close by on the counter, in a covered small calabash, she found the boiled baby cassava that went with it. She opened them side by side, her mouth springing as their aromas collided, the cassava flat and cold, the corned beef barely body-warm, richly tanged of olive oil. She broke one bit and dipped it in the other, and took a taste and, hunger adding relish, judged it excellent going down. Halfway through the feast, she remembered to sit. Then, for the lull, life seemed afloat in satisfaction.

Done eating, and in contemplation with a satisfied stomach of how well Seyeh still stirred his pot-spoon, a burp rose to remark on the burnt-garlic flavour of the olive oil generously over the cassava. Stretching arms hard and long, Uxann pushed out her great chest in support of the observation. She yawned restlessly, growled, "Yeah! Grrreat," and peered about the gloom for something to do.

Through the slits of the windows' boards, clear slivers of sky leaked into the kitchen space. Curious about the brightness, she went to the wall-post where the clock hung. But he had neglected to wind it. It had gone silent sometime five minutes to seven. The widest crack between the boards showed insufficient sky for an estimate. So then she couldn't anymore skirt the idea. She had to go in the yard to see the sky, to check the time, because the clock wasn't working. A need that was real, a logic reasonable. After all, it wasn't daylight—a main point of his note, maybe the main point. For certain sake, she pussyfooted to the dining table and checked Seyeh's note. A fair reading, after which there seemed no objections to a walk in the yard. In the night. And for very good reason.

▼▼▼

SHE FILLED HER lungs with the cool, silvery brightness, her bare feet cringing on the gritty ground. Shifting to a kinder spot, she pulled the big dress close and looked about as if for the first time. She was almost hidden in the shadow of the house, the sky shining so brightly, leaves shimmering as though polished, and straight up, stars white and tiny, their winking cold. There must be some fullmoon, she thought, and started around for the other side of the house.

Coolest, softest moonshine streaming the air, it had just topped the forest. Silvery world, unreachable queen, she commanded the glowing night-sky, a kowtow of clouds crowding just far back enough for contrast. So close, Uxann could see clear detail—the sea of tranquillity, the something mountains. She pulled her clothes tighter about her, rocking sideways as she breathed in the beauty.

So this is the jewelry womankind craved, Uxann mused, recalling Keah's story about periods. All asudden, she longed for Keah, wished for her confidential presence to hear Uxann respond to that base hankering, of her sympathy for the thrall.

After a while she began a stroll about the yard. In the garden there were still some pigeon peas to pick. And some peppers. And some tomatoes. And, on the fence behind the peppers, she could make out the knobby pale green of at least two corrily. Paps had been slacking up, she thought: Perhaps this was the work he put off to manage his new schedules.

Farther along the fence side, she found a full cucumber. She hefted and plucked it, and added it to the basket of her skirt—without realizing, she had pouched it to hold harvest. Then she stepped squishily on a fallen overripe one, the start from the squirminess nearly taking her heart away as thoughts of longfellows slithered through her mind. Her sneakers on, before she was

done, there were two loads of vegetables on the counter
of the outside kitchen.

The guava tree at the corner of the land was laden.
Pinkish even in the liquid moonlight, ripe ones hung
low, the scent of them heavy. She wandered under,
looking up, lingering, before picking her choice. And
just the delight she expected, which, as she peacefully
munched, provided a notion: Maybe this night-living
wouldn't be too bad.

There were three hens' nests Paps had missed, seven
eggs in all. Mr. Mongoose, too, had missed them up to
now. Uxann pouched his further chances. She also rescued two muddy duck eggs. Then it was another trip to
the kitchen counter.

She had been saving the zebus for last. Now in the
warmth of their bulk, she was first content just to stand
and breathe in their rich, sweet funk. She was next to
Boobee, the troublesome cow. With firm, scratching
fingers, Uxann furrowed the hide against the hair's
grain, then smoothed out the disarray, over and over.
She rubbed her cheek to the zebu's neck, and felt the
grind of its patient cuds—a rhythm strong, infectious.
She roughed the cow's hide in the slow tempo. Gradually moving down the neck, her body following.
Down the belly sameway. Then around the backsides.
Stop to stroke the tail. Then a stoop, and she was hidden
in between them. Safe, so she could get down to the

udders she sought. And secure in the craving to kneel
down in comfort, slip the long teat in, and suck and
slobber to her fill.

When she got back in, it was toilet, then bed. She was
soon fast asleep, clean forgetting the thank-you note
she'd intended for Paps.

▼▼▼

SHE AWOKE TO a humid morning; from the dull light
through the curtain, skies were probably grey. She sat
up and listened to the house, it seeming all to her. Then
listened again at her door for a moment before quietly
opening it and peering about. At the table, no note.
Then at the shoe box, Paps' favorite working boots
gone. She was alone.

She returned to her room and gingerly pulled the
posie from under her bed. Then, careful of too much
sloshing, she took it to the toilet bowl and emptied it.
She washed and returned it under her bed. Then she did
her toilette, stared in the mirror some, before starting
for the kitchen to see what day had for her.

▼▼▼

ONE AFTERNOON, CLOSE to the edge of dreaming, a distant laughter called to mind that school had recently re-opened. Her heart quickened as complications from the thought tried to mass. But she fell off into a doze just before they engulfed her.

▼▼▼

JUST AFTER SOME other midday, outside the air was sultry in quiet submission to the heat. Although it wasn't so bad in the curtained house, with the cool kept in. Uxann had napped and woken with a yen for chocolate. So she lit a clean dry-wood fire and made a potful in milk. Absently, expertly, she was pouring from one cup to another, cooling it down, when she suddenly missed her mark and spilled a splatter on the counter. Her name was being furtively hailed: "Uxann . . . Uxann . . ."

She stopped dead and put down the cup. Then, on

silent tiptoe, she went to the window with the back-garden view. Eye to the biggest crack, she glimpsed the skirt of a uniform, and her heart welled to happy tears. Some girls from school had come to visit her! Someone called again, "Uxann. I hope you ent sleeping. We hear you sick bad, and quarantined, and such. We come to say hello. Is me, Eralee, and Miata, and . . ."

Uxann gently cleared her nose into her sleeve, and sniffed. She had recognized the voice, though. Only Eralee would relish saying "quarantine" so.

A new voice alerted, "Yuh smelling hot chocolate?"

"Ah think so, yu'know."

The alert one again. "Ah bet she in there cooking . . ." She continued too low-toned for Uxann to hear. But it was snide. The others' burst of hearty laughter proved it. Someone sweetened the joke by repeating, "Is that what sicken she? . . . Is that what really do it? . . ." The banter pinching her to the quick.

Then Eralee broke in, "Allyuh behave, nuh. Is true, oui, 'what's joke for man is death for crapaud.' Look how the girl sick unto death in dere, and allyuh skinning teeth out here."

The laughter calmed to a few defiant sniggers. Someone—sounded like Miss Alert again—suggested practically, "Well, we come for guava. So leh we pick guava, huh. What allyuh say?"

Must have passed quorum. Further sounds became grunty efforts of a guava raid. Thoughtfully, Uxann retreated to her room with the rest of the chocolate. The whole episode grated her grain—the gall of them, their heartlessness. And Paps . . . ! So she was sick and quarantined, huh? That's how he had explained her absence in school, huh? She sank onto the bed, sipped her tepid chocolate. "Quarantined by a strange growth." That should be the name of her sickness, she thought bitterly. Whatever else of the rumour, though, it made one thing definite. For reputation and pride, she could not ever be seen. Even in the night she had to be careful. For herself, for Paps' slick explanations.

▼▼▼

ONCE THE GUAVA was finished, the group of girls stopped coming by. Don't miss them, Uxann told herself harshly, they only come for guava, and to laugh at me. She was living at night anyhow. Didn't really want to keep up with day business, and dull school business at that. Nah. She didn't miss them at all. They used to come by afternoons. Now, instead of shifting her time around their visits, she tried to sleep.

▼▼▼

MINDFUL BUT HELPLESS to the whim, one night—skirt
like a tent around her belly—she dressed in uniform and
walked the long graveled road to school. She found the
main gate locked and chained. Leaning on it, by the
scant light she studied the bare schoolyard, trying to
imagine herself in line-up. Then she wondered, Why
lock the gate at night? At all? What were they keeping
in, or out? And what if the school had eyes that could
see her now, and tell? Suddenly, she felt observed, and
skulked away as fast as her big belly allowed.

▼▼▼

MIGHT'VE BEEN A quick-doze dream, or a plain day-
dream. But one afternoon, in the outside kitchen, she
heard a girl's voice, messaging. Flinching at the brilliance, Uxann tried to see through the cracks, but the
girl was in a blind spot. So taken with trying to sight

her, Uxann missed the first part of her story. Although, she might have anyhow, for, as if in a race against time, the girl was running her mouth mile a minute:

". . . fill the space up. So dey take she to town to de fix-up man, an' dey pay wit'out smiles de pound and de crown de man charge, an' dey get she gap fill up nice-nice. Only ting. Now she come back, de new teeth can't stay fixed. She can't eat. She can't talk. She can't whistle, dey shiftin'. She can only keep dem in to grin. An' nothin' can crack her to smile. She vex, vex all the time, keepin' to she self. Dey say since she new fixtures, gap-tooth Jainee come more stiff-neck. . . ."

Time was up, though. The story stopped, and the unknown teller ran away.

▼▼▼

A HUMID DAY that had her feeling cooped up like a feast-day fowl. Tired and sluggish with her belly growing cumbersome, she hardly left the bed. Except for the necessary trips to kitchen and toilet, she drowsed through the hours, hollowing her mind to suit the hushed house, awaiting Paps' arrival so that, with him located, she could get out and start her night. Breathe some fresh air. Take a walk. Sleep took her, though.

Much later, she awoke in alarm, aware of absence. She hadn't heard the creaking kitchen door, the crash of his boots in the shoe box—the usual announcements of his arrival. Uneasiness for energy, she quicked to the door, opened it softly, and held her breath. No sound of him in the darkness. Quiet and anxious, she checked through the house. He was not there.

She used the toilet, then returned to her room and sat on the bed's edge, worrying the sheet with sweaty palms. Where was he? The question wouldn't let her sit. Time and again it spurred her to her window to crack the curtain and confirm how late it was. Where could he be at this hour? In her belly, the baby squirmed. And then a treacherous idea wormed into her mind: What if he had abandoned her?

All asudden her room was too small and hot. The baby twisted violently. She rushed to the kitchen to peer out through the ugly curtains on the track side of the house. No sign of him! She rushed back to her restive bed, trying to catch her runaway breath, think past her crowding panic. Her belly writhed sideways. She felt mindless, stupid as slops. Then the *clack!* of the kitchen door being unlatched cracked the ominous stillness and made her jump. And in relief she collapsed on the worrisome bed and muffled her crying in the pillow. The baby kicked.

▼▼▼

ANOTHER DOZE, ANOTHER dream: She has died making an angel, and is on her way to heaven, seated securely in a scented rocking chair made entirely of flower petals, sliding up winding liana vines, whisking through the upper forest levels like a hummingbird, past the whistling birds' kingdom, past the small fruit-eaters' preserves, then the beautiful bigger boss-birds—the hawks, the eagles, Gabilan—and as she passes, everyone is so peaceful, they hullo her with approving eyes and welcome whistles and displays of their beautiful feathers . . . then suddenly, just as she is approaching heaven's sky proper, where she will be able at last to float happy above the tumult, just as she is about to reach herself out of the sweet-scented chair, the angel, her baby, appears in front of her, paddling the air with a shiny sword, grinning terrible pointed teeth, barring the way, and actually swinging at her . . . what else to do? . . . she scrambles out of the flower-chair, and starts down its liana pulley, sliding down crabwise trying to outpace the angel-baby who is gleefully lopping off the liana arm's length by arm's length, chopping faster and faster, and getting closer to her, his flying sword clattering through the ever-shortening vine . . .

▼▼▼

SHE AWOKE TO a rattle from the galvanized roof above. The rattle of a bit of wood, or a stone someone had thrown up on the roof so it'd roll and rouse a sleeper. Uxann rose and was swift to the outside kitchen, and to the cracks glimpsing out the back of the house.

Faint on the air, diminishing, a clinking. Might it be a jingle of bracelets on a wrist flung carefree? Uxann rushed from one light-sliver to the other, exploring every bit of her splintered view, but whoever it was had given up and gone.

The flush of disappointment drained her to a sudden tiredness that recalled her bed with its twisted dream. Still, the thought of bed was warm, and welcoming. First, a drink of water. She picked up the calabash and poured from the earthen pitcher. And the bitter in her mouth did wash away some with each cool swallow.

As Uxann replaced the calabash on the counter, an unfamiliar nudge and rustle from its usual spot caused her to look down. A folded brown paper was sticking through a crack in the boards; hidden behind the calabash, and at that low level, it was too out of the way as a peephole. She pulled the paper through and unfolded it, and, with a swell of joy, recognized the handwriting. She read:

Is me, your friend in sickness. Is only resently I fine out about your aflikshun and how you so contagous from the horse's mouth. Well girl, every star I see fall, I wishing with my eyes close tight for the best recovery for you. And these nights I watching the sky a lot. So don't worry too much. Sinse I hear I pass two three times but every try I fine the house quiet like a gravestone. So I suppoze you resting a lot. And that maybe good for some sickness. Well anyhow, I stick this message in this crease here behind your speschul goblet, cause is only Miss Rainwater you who wood move your calabash and expose it. So I hoping is so it go, and only you set eyes on these words. For you well know my trouble if not. So you see why I cant write any thing strate out plane, and why I have to sine off now.

So keep a brave hart. Your frend is wishing well for you.

                    XXXX

Pacing the kitchen, then her room, sitting on the bed, Uxann re-read the letter ten, twenty times, teary-eyed smiling, re-spelling the words, puzzling at meanings, ever-savouring the deep comfort of the message. Keah was thinking of her. Her friend was constant.

▼▼▼

FULLMOON NIGHT, AND Uxann with no special destination, just exploring to waste time and savour the moon-
lit vista. With the muted brilliance, out in the open she
could see clear as day up to fifty or so yards. Under the
forest's canopy, vision was sharp only a short distance.
But going slowly and keeping eyes peeled, unfright-
ened, she moved her bulk along with lithe, certain steps,
ceaselessly gleaning the gloom for the subtle action going on: the bat flitting from fruit near the spine; the
fluffed-up sleeping bird atwitch on its perch; the acrid
urine of some animal's spoor. All at once, unplanned,
into the darkness she yelled, "Big belly!" and felt that
notion safely absorbed. Then clearly, but not so loud,
she called, "Mama!" and waited.

She concentrated, expectant. Not pitying, or sad, or
anything, all remained unfazed in her great, fat forest
with its big fat-trunked trees of rough barks and low
buttress-roots she could lean and rest her fat belly on.
Her cool, easy forest went on unchanged, its traces
and creeks and creatures unsleeping that fluttered and
shrilled and hooted and hummed.

She flopped for a rest against a tree trunk that didn't mind her heaviness, didn't feel weighed down. A mosquito buzzed invisibly, pesky as the thought: How would my mother treat me? How would she handle this situation? But Uxann could conjure no sense of her mother, no mood to cypher from, so the question's purpose emptied.

She gazed at a gloomy stand of slim, silver-skinned saplings just off the track. Impulsively, she rushed over and clasped her arms about one that was medium-sized and, belly jamming, danced it to the sway of breeze, scuffing her sneakers on the leaf-strewn floor. As dark-green leaf-curtains rippled, round and round she danced in her private parlour. A grand hall bestrewn with delicate night-shades—pale and slender, or shimmering palm-shapes, all defending her from the glare of daylight eyes that would see her only as fat and big-bellied. Which maybe she was, except that here in her palace of nurturing forest, more important was how she fitted in, how she felt close, a mother herself.

▼▼▼

SHE WAS ALONE, stealing about the drowsy afternoon house on tiptoe as if some terror would be released by any hasty noise. At his door, she paused to test, and it swung open to the slight push. He had curtained his windows, too, with the rough, ugly drapes. His small table was bare, his chair neatly placed square under it. The dull-coloured insides of the stagnant curtains over their ever-closed windows reminded her of peeping at the toddlers playing dangerously in the sand. She never saw them anymore. Behind the shroud, she was the entertainment now. The strayed and condemned one. Their faces masked, the windows watched her through six square glass eyes. Six crosswise gaps that sneered, "Shame! Shame!" until Uxann shrank out of his room and fled blameworthy, ranging her deserved sepulcher. Then, as she took the step down to the outside kitchen, she brushed against his musty raincoat, and the smell of it set her weeping.

That night, brushing with her mixture of baking soda and ember ash, her teeth reminded of his broad smile, bright with mischief too much for a big man.

EYES SEE MORE slowly in the dark, they need help. Ears have to come in, nose must up its part, the whole body must show caution. In the dark, Mankind must learn from Night's creatures. Not so much bat as common cat. From shadows and shades, too, and predator and prey. Stalking slow or swiftly escaping, night animals live patterns in their pace. Miss or pounced on, they survive or die in a rhythm—whether they rush about, or wait and watch while Nature teaches them their Fate. Many a nice night, holding her belly, feeling it live, Uxann, too, took lessons.

Once, well past midnight, she watched him come home. It might've been a payday night. Stilled a sharper quiet by the shock, she recognized him from under cover of a low-branched tree, watching him anew with longing eyes—how smoothly he walked the path, picking his way home, light on his feet to almost dancing, yet his eyes sharply about, this way and that, an exciting spice to his manner. He looked a risk, smooth as any young man—at least, any of the male teachers in school. Like Mr. Roland, famous for ever looking to play punt 'n' crick with the big girls.

As Uxann appraised Paps afresh, a sudden sense blinked on the situation with him and Keah. Not so much that Keah was forward and hot, she admitted, but that *he* was a graceful man. His eyes were bright, his vigour strong, girls could fall for him.

Just as he was about to enter the open field to the backyard track—a mere twenty feet away—he stopped short and turned, gaze searching the area in which she felt so confidently hidden. Full around, he turned. Long and hard, he bored into the darkness. Still as a rock, all atremble in her mind, for a terrible moment she thought he'd approach. But then he cocked his head, dismissing, and strode on to the back-garden track and into the house. Churning with relief and regret, she stared at the door, pulled shut, unlatched, as if his image had remained on it.

Recalled by some sound, Uxann sighed and faded farther into the night. She couldn't go home now, not with him prowling the house. From an aimless meander, she found herself on her school-time shortcut track and realized her destination. Keeping a slow, steady pace she went off the shortcut a few yards from her usual entry spot into Dosaro's. The weak moonlight paled the graveled road to a vague curved swath diffusing into the massive shadow of surrounding forest. Other than the clouds brisk across the moon, she seemed the only thing moving.

One hand in care of her tear-droop belly, she climbed down the two-foot embankment and stepped across the flood drain. From there she surveyed the width of waist-high elephant-grass to the fence, night-light and breeze waving it like silvery fur. Anything long and bad-lucky might be lurking in the hairs of that grass. But this far come, she couldn't stop. So, with halt-and-search step, she ventured her sneakers into the grass. Ten thousand racing heartbeats later, safe at the entry spot, her anxiety was turned jaunty. With a stoop and a squeeze, the belly was no problem through the shifted stave. All of it worthwhile under the arbour's canopy, where the darkness was soft, and the air warm and vapoury. Nightshades or no, night after night, just as gone days, she returned to the security there.

▼▼▼

ANOTHER NIGHT, BEING invisible in the broadleaf shadows of the new banana stool sprung up by the duck pond, Uxann felt a presence arrive. Animal of some sort, close outside the fence; she immediately located its lair in a dense clump of bushes. Once the start of awareness passed, though, her instincts were unalarmed, and she adjusted her ken to accommodate the creature.

Some time later, a suppressed snort from the bushes returned her from deep thoughts, and she remembered the lurking animal. But her bladder demanded inside, and she went, dismissing her immediate curiosity. Then, as it was getting cool anyhow, she remained in her room.

▼▼▼

Several nights later, about the same time, the animal came again to its lair under the dense bush just outside the duck pond. Uxann heard its peculiar cough and, thinking she must've discovered its night's route, relaxed the same way, without anxiety. It wasn't long before she fled inside, though, as the weather turned to pre-dawn drizzles.

▼▼▼

Returning from a shortcut stroll, she passed near the dense spot the animal had chosen for lair. Just as she decided to drift that way for a better examination, there came that suppressed snort. Not so much warning as notice, it seemed to declare, "I'm here!" Uxann got back on track for the garden-gate.

Still, the night serene, she gave the duck pond a visit to sit on her old box. She did the usual—looked at the stars, braided her hair, disturbed a sleeping duck family huddled in their sandbox corner. That earned half-hearted hisses from the mama, a few automatic peeps from one displaced duckling. Then it was all quiet night once again.

Vague movement pulled her eyes across to the dog-like creature leaving. High-haunched, dark-coated, deliberately in the open, letting her see, it slunk slowly away.

▼▼▼

THE TASTE OF her leisurely raid on Dosaro's still tying up her tongue, Uxann crossed a dried-up ravine and entered a trace through a copse of dense high woods. The deeper shade, like a dark-green umbrella of mottled moods, sharpened her senses, attuned her to the quiet. Alert that unseen business was proceeding per usual around her intrusion, Uxann stepped carefully, stingy about lending full weight to searching for smooth track.

She thought of the forest's eyes minding their own affairs, and hers. She was just passing through, she wanted to assure them. Aware that the path was alive and could hurt, she was watching closely each step, and being careful of offending in these natural woods, where every size found place, and every kind, even ill-fated her, counted.

First chance, though, she got out of that thrilling briar-patch and back to the brighter, common trail, going along more casually now, munching more sour-sweet fruit, guzzling it down with relish. Reaching into her bulging skirt-pocket for another pomme-rac, she stopped short.

What was that sound? Up in front, wasn't that a barking carried on the wind?

Uxann braced against a trunk, and closed her eyes to better ascertain. *Yip! Yip! Yip!* it came flying on the air. Then an answering chorus. Then a howl—*no!* howls. Many of them. Dogs! The frenzied yelps of a hunting pack on the trail—and big-belly she in their way! Pomme-rac forgotten, heart suddenly drumming alarm, she leaned against the tree trunk, and clasped her pumpkin belly.

Flushed by the racket, Uxann abandoned the shortcut and cut into the black, scratchy hazard of sidebush, angling well away from the pack's approach. The going was hard here, spikes of sparse underbrush surprising with pokes at almost every step. Her arms, groping forward for guidance and protection, were entangled by small hanging vines, invisible in the night, some with prickles. In short order, she was boxed in by the bush, and stopped altogether, panting. Should she reverse steps? She peered about, ears straining, trying to locate herself and rein a wild desperation. Trapped in the tangle, and the frantic pack was close enough to catch the harsh gargle in their snarls!

Panicked, left hand on her belly, right like a sword, she ran blindly from the yelping din into the entrapping thicket. Wasn't long before it stumbled her over a long-fallen log. She snatched at yielding fronds for balance, but capsized belly-first on hard ground. While, fixed on their business, as if on an open track alongside, the baying dog-pack went furiously racing past. A pain cold and fierce down her hips seized so strong, it twisted off her chagrin at panicking so foolishly, and spun her dizzily smaller and smaller down a velveteen whirl.

▼▼▼

. . . A COARSE FILE on soft meat, gnawing away, scraping, scraping, lick after lick on her calf . . . a rough warm towel washing her leg, firmly rubbing as it needed to, sometimes so rough it didn't soothe anymore . . . she pulled the foot away, shifted from right

side to her back, and woke into a terrific dizziness . . .
relaxing into the swoon as the warm washcloth returned to her calf, advancing over her knee, intending
further . . .

▼▼▼

. . . THICK, HAIRY, WET, a paw! . . . pulling, scratching
her calf timidly, but insistent . . . claws scraped harsh at
her knee as a heavy breathing changed position next to
her, and with a start Uxann was alerted to the great
doglike shape scampering away, tongue hanging bash-
fully . . . she touched her temple, which ached to bursting. Pain elsewhere, too, mainly about her belly and
hips; she gentled the areas with her fingers, certifying
the pain, soothing the pangs. She shifted slightly, rustling her forest-bed. After a moment, like answer, a
stifled animal sneeze came close from the darkened
bushes. She swooned again . . .

▼▼▼

. . . A SHARP DISCOMFORT ruled her belly; to her hands it seemed lumps were wrestling under the hot, tight skin. A muckiness there drew attention to her fancy. But when she moved her legs to reach, it stung down there, and a deeper, different pain set in. A pain that called for urgent home. She sat up and, mid-swoon, grabbed a sapling beside her to haul herself upright. The effort nearly sagged her back down, but with it, a warm smell arose—a blood-and-brine scent she recognized from birthing yard animals she had tended. And Uxann knew her own had begun, forced too soon, and in the dark dangerous forest. She had to get herself home.

Bracing on tree trunks, grabbing at fronds and saplings, any and everything an aid, she tottered about bewildered: Where was her familiar shortcut track? Every step slicked the cooling muck between her legs. Every step jarred her tender belly. Panic was seeping back. She so meandering away precious time, and so needful of getting home! She closed her eyes, took a deep draught, and marshaled her swimming mind. *Think!* she commanded, clutching the thick of a branch.

The sniffling cough of the strange beast came, off to the right now. Instinct caught at the suggestion, opened her eyes, and set her towards it—and the shortcut was right there. She peered along the track, making it familiar again, visualizing the dimmed way, all the while containing the pain she'd walk home. Then she set foot to the struggle.

▼▼▼

. . . THE BLOOD-LICKING BRUTE there all the way, sometimes vanished to a rustle alongside in the bush, sometimes up ahead, big, doggish, apause. The pathway shimmering strangely, the black, stable tree trunks shifting about, falling flat like fence-posts to high wind. Uxann focused on the brute dog, somewhere real to aim her feet on the wavering track. . . .

. . . pain flared in her loins, distressed her to stop the while to manage it, until, with gritting it down, she could set to again, with the big beast as a steady mark, directing her stepping feet, her hands a worry-basket of fingers bearing this tender, leaky belly along a track of sudden-risen roots, writhing up out of the ground, intending to trick and trip her down. Unless she rested, paused to recover, and then might have lost her bearings, except for the doggish beast farther along, a fixed level to measure by, and sidle carefully over each reaching root trap, hardly raising her feet, all the bend in the knees and none in the hips, any careless bend a calling bell to the pain-demons ever ready for extra duty. All the wicked road they were so hard-working, hardly resting then working hard again, forcing her pauses more regularly so she could cool down the pain by pulling in deeper breaths of night air. Then starting the hard way once again, landmarking by the constant beast-dog . . .

▼▼▼

. . . FOG-MINDED ABOUT HER progress to it, the outside kitchen door was there, the top half unlatched and swung open. She hung over the bottom half-door, marshaling intentions. Unhook the door and swing it open. But the rest against the door eased the pain somehow, and she loathed giving up the relief, even to get inside. So she just rested there, and let peacefulness overcome her . . .

▼▼▼

. . . WARM . . . ON HER own familiar bed . . . and the
pain coming about to recharge, again rising . . . and she
could bear it no more . . . blankness swept over . . .

▼▼▼

. . . HER SLACK HEAD supported, a pushy cup gentle
at her lips. "Drink! Get some down yuh throat, Girl
Chile!" Paps' voice, raspy with concern. Tears of relief
welling, Uxann slurped awkwardly at the warm liquid.
Then, but for the tiniest trickling down her throat, the
world went grey again . . .

▼▼▼

. . . ALL THE LONG night that's what she'd missed: Amid this thought, she emerged from the fog to the scent of him against her face—raw soap, strong coffee, and sweated work-clothes—and relaxed right away, neck cradled on his arm. It was all right now. Paps'd take care of everything.

"Get dis kaya down, Girl Chile!" Urgent, persuading, his low voice edged on, "We have donkey-work to do, and dis go make de pain less stubborn."

Whatever you say, Paps, she smiled in her mind, and arranged her lips to slurp again. She got a good bit; warm, but tongue-twisty bitter, the brew went down. Then he allowed her head back to the cool pillow . . .

▼▼▼

. . . HER HEAD DRIFTING, she reached a hand up to steady it and nearly missed. At her own touch, she realized that

actually, all of her was light, maybe delicately afloat a
half-inch above the smooth, cool bed-sheet. She raised
reluctant lids and slowly blinked around, assessing the
room. It seemed steady enough. The worst monster of
the pain-army—a battle-loving, off-and-on devil in her
belly—was on retreat and resting up again. Overall, she
wasn't feeling too bad, though there seemed to be something so absurd about such a cheery notion that she
sniggered. Not too hard, since it caused a spasm down
her belly.

Paps came in. From out of sight at the door, he asked,
"How yuh feeling?" his voice a cave's echo.

"Not too bad," she answered. Then, hearing nothing, she realized that her mouth had not opened. Trying
again, she forced out, "Okay," and tried to smile reas-
surance.

He loomed into view, face far away over her, eyebrows bunched in concern. He boomed again, "Don't
worry 'bout how yuh seeing things. Is de kaya what
working. Yuh understanding me?"

He looked down at her, the middle of his black, black
eyes growing larger and swirling slowly.

"Yuh understanding me, Girl Chile?" he said. It
sounded like a funny line she'd heard before, and she
giggled.

"Listen to me, Uxann. Ah know yuh could hear me.
So listen close."

Suppressing the humour of his seriousness, Uxann said, "Yes, boss." And again, she couldn't stop giggling.

"Uxann. Uxann. Hear me. The morning getting on. Ah have to go set up de men tasks. Ah will be soon back. Take a sip of dis on de table off and on, and yuh go be all right. Yuh pains far apart. Nothing should happen before ah come back. Okay? Yuh understand me?"

She had loosely followed his talking at the start, but became distracted by how his eyebrows scrunched up to strengthen his points. Nevertheless, to amuse him, she said, "Yes, boss."

He fierced eyes at her, making more furrows with his brows. "A sip off and on will keep de pain away," he rumbled. Then his workboots trampled the floorboards on their way out.

And she was aswim in her peaceful whorl . . .

▼▼▼

. . . THE PAIN WAS a trapped fire-bird in the cage of her belly, trying hard to get out. It flapped and thrashed about, its heartbeat a throbbing bass drum, intent on winning the struggle. It would kill if it had to. And she wanted to die, yet it wouldn't pull tight her final knot, only kept squeezing downwards in waves that weakened her bladder, so that each time it made battle, she was helplessly dribbling pee. She felt that if she could walk a little, it'd give her ease. But the pain at her waist so weakened her, she couldn't heave herself from the bed. So she squirmed into a tight tremble and tried not to groan. Although she couldn't stop a thin *"hnnnnnnn"* of a whine that seeped out between her clenched teeth. And each time, right at her limit, when it had grown uncontainable, the pain would rest, and Uxann would be lulled gradually so comfortable, it seemed certain she'd manage the next attack. Until it swelled burst again.

Then Uxann heard the kitchen's half-door slam open, and Paps' boots thump to her door. And he was at her side in two stomps. "How yuh feeling?"

"Pain, Paps," she grunted. "It really strong."

"It coming regular?"

"I don't know, Paps," said Uxann.

"Yuh take any of de kaya tea?"

"No. I forget where it is."

He cradled her head up, and put the cup to her lips so she could sip the lukewarm brew. "Dis'd make yuh relax," he said, "and de pain won't be so bad."

Believing him, she closed her eyes and breathed deeply, and waited.

"Ah going heat some hot water," Paps said. "Is not long now." Then he thumped out of the room.

▼▼▼

THE PAUSES BETWEEN were next to nothing now, the pain itself different and so powerful that Uxann abandoned her vow of silence and groaned out loud. It soothed her belly somehow, so she groaned again. Then even louder as the pain screwed deeper in.

Paps tromped into the room breathing running-hard. "What happening?" he demanded hoarsely.

"It coming, Paps! Right now." Uxann gasped in a breath. "I making it right now."

Paps stared at her. She had never seen his face so confused, his eyes—even stale drunk—so red and wild. Rocking slightly side to side, he shook his finger at her. "Now we for it. Yuh see what stubbornness bring? Yuh see what yuh cause, huh? Girl Chile, huh? See what yuh do?"

But so quick, already the pain, fierce as fire, was rested and returned. Middle moan, Uxann pleaded, "Please, Paps. Not now. Something coming down, in truth. It coming out."

He grimaced sourly, squinting his eyes as if a sudden hot light had blinded him. "Well, all right then," he said decisively, and hustled from the room.

▼▼▼

WITH EVERY PANG now, there was also an urge to force down on the mass in her belly. Like a giant constipation, it seemed impossibly large, too great to push out. Yet it was moving. She found that with each pause of the pain, if she took a deep reinforcing breath, the need to force down in her belly was kinder, the sharp agony clean and easier.

Meantime, Paps was busying around, now with a damp cloth at her forehead, now clasping her hand as she strained and pushed. All the time he muttered, carrying on fussily as if in conversation:

"This is shame. Deep shame."

"You is a stubborn girl."

"Is yuh mother blood in you. Dat's what it is."

"I treat you human, and you treat me mangy dog."

Then there came a powerful, particular pain, cramping in her lower belly, stretching and stinging at her fancy, and Uxann knew the baby was getting out. "Quick,

Paps," she gasped, and squatted her legs wide apart, "it coming out. Pull it out."

And he was down there, hauling up her dress, busy with the warm, wet, soothing cloths. Then, distress in his eyes, he was back at her face. "Shame, Girl Chile, shame! Look what it doing you," he cried, "look how it hurting you."

Uxann glared at him, seized of impatience and defiance. Why was he jigging around so, when *she* was suffering the blood and pee and nastiness? Why was he wasting time talking shame and worrying with shyness when *she* was in this tremendous pain? She just wanted that thing out of her, wanted the pain ended. And right then, with a force of its own, and mightier than any before, a terrible agony sliced her. "Oh, God. Seyeh. Take it out!" she screamed.

He was bent down there, touching, helping the baby slip out. All at once the pressure went away, the pain miraculously done to a gentle hurt. Almost nothing at all. So blissful, she could sleep.

Vaguely, she saw Paps rise up holding something. There was the clink and snip of scissors, then a gasp and a sort of wheezing. Then Paps put the wet, slippery, squirming thing on her bosom, and drew her arms around to embrace it close.

"It come too soon. Is a small baby, but is a complete boy," he pronounced, voice proud as if he'd just made it himself. Suddenly, dreadfully tired, without a look at the baby on her breast, Uxann closed her eyes . . .

▼▼▼

. . . PAPS WAS PRESSING down on her stomach. "Force out de afterbirth," he insisted. "Is only a little bit more."

She pushed and felt something slippery pass out of her. With slight alarm, she reached her free hand down to catch it. But Paps had gathered it into the warm towel. She got the smell, though, like soured zebu cream, or fresh blood with a stinky-sweet tang. Then she fell asleep.

▼▼▼

SHE AWOKE IN comfort, immediately aware of her soothed fancy padded up as when she had her period. There was no real pain anywhere. Neither noise nor sweat. She reached both hands down, feeling her unfamiliar, so-soft, new-flattened belly. She was pressing flab gingerly when Paps came into the room. He held the bundled-up child in his hands, and was trying hard to keep his face straight, kept tossing shiny glances from the bundle of baby to her, and back again. Then he caught Uxann's eyes and grinned, proud and boyish, just as she liked.

"It come too soon," he said reassuringly, "but it strong. It small, but strong. Complete in form and healthy. And it not bawling, don't cry at all. Is a bullock yuh make, Girl Chile."

Eyes soft, smile broad, Paps gazed down at her. He put the baby in the crook of her arm, with the head near her breast. He said, "It have a dent on de side where ah grab he head to pull, but dat will soon level out. And he little bit blue. But dat is all right. He strong. He lungs clear. Once yuh start nursing 'im, some morning sun will clean out he blood."

"Nursing him?" The idea echoed in her mind foolishly, elbowing aside her astonishment at his confidence and camaraderie, only another dollop on her own sweet happiness.

". . . hurting?" Paps had asked.

"Not much," she answered. "Is more like I numb all over."

"Yuh all right. Yuh young and strong. Yuh go survive, and he go survive for certain. He is a fighter. Yuh shoulda seen 'im come out, hand fist tight, ready to fight, he head turning, one eye open under de veil, peeping to make sure. Is a fighter yuh make, girl. Little as he is, yuh shoulda see 'im struggle to pull breath. Oh, he's a striver for certain, dis one."

Paps so sounded like a fan at a game, Uxann searched his face as it stared at the bundle beside her. She had to mention it. "Paps. Ah sorry I shame you so."

With furrowed brow, he fixed damp, bright eyes on her. "Don't bring up dat time no more, okay. History start now. Is from now on we counting. Ah don't care no more about who, how, and when. Ah don't care if frog spawn 'im, Girl Chile. Now is you and me and he. Alone, we starting over altogether."

Eyes locked into hers, he nodded agreement out of her. And even though she felt something contrary lurking under the surface of her happiness, she said, "Okay, Paps."

Paps continued to nod absently. "But yuh have to hold yuh baby. Yuh have to cuddle 'im," he said.

There was a sharp little hurt in her belly when she turned, so with careful movements she picked up the quiet, swaddled baby, and examined the face. "Oh, Paps! It ugly!" she exclaimed with surprise. The face was a squinched-up, wrinkled thing that didn't seem new at all. "Paps, look at it," she repeated. "Like it old already. It ugly, in truth."

Except that as she spoke, this impression lessened.

For, looking past the run of dribble aside its mouth, Uxann caught the tiny glints under dark well-formed eyebrows, eyes that blinked how indeed new and un-placed it felt, and how desperately helpless it was, and in need, being so unshielded to everything. And just like that, her feeling changed towards her new baby, and thinking how weak and lost it was, she held it close, comforting it against her breast.

"Yes. That's de ticket," Paps encouraged. "Put a teat in de mouth. Make it suckle."

Starting to reach for her great hard breasts, Uxann hesitated and regarded Seyeh shyly. "Paps!!!" she pro-tested, unable to say more.

Paps had the idea, though. With a chuckle, he started from the room. "No shame involved," he said. "Right now, yuh is but a bag o' milk to 'im."

Alone, she held the baby in position, and slipped the teat—embarrassingly big as a fingertip—into its ready mouth, where it fitted like it was grooved for, and in-stantly the baby was attached and suckling strong.

▼▼▼

GONE WAS HER empty time. Feeding and caring for the baby, keeping it from crying and clean, occupied Uxann's every hour. Plain greedy, or forever hungry, it seemed permanently attached to her breasts, suckling her ready flow like a zangee, and by the first few days was showing the result. The wrinkled skin was filling out, the features—high nose, thick eyebrows—prominent. And the blue-green tint under the fragile skin? To Paps' instructions, every morning Uxann sat behind the east window's new curtains—thin white ones he had hung. And the filtered early sunlight was steadily fading the off-colour away.

For Uxann herself, the lighter house was a major sign that Paps had returned to her. Right after the baby came—the second day, maybe—he had replaced the horror-brown vine curtains with fine, lacy ones. Still resettling into this daylight world, she watched him work without comment, but Paps was getting back to his talkative way.

"Let de maccoes beat dis!" he proclaimed with satisfied chuckles. "Once it bright outside, light could come in without bringing maccoe eyes with it. And if it bright inside, is only moving shadows maccoe seeing."

More taken by his energy than science, Uxann's nod was automatic to his pause. But reading it that she was close following, Paps triumphantly declared, "So, Girl Chile, behind dem daylight windows, yuh safe from meddlers like yuh been hid in a mirror!"

It made no sense to her whatsoever, yet Uxann put a smile to her nodding. Then the baby saved her from more with its demand whimper, and, still unable to bare herself in his presence, she excused herself to her room to nurse.

▼▼▼

THE UNDERSIDE TO this good time, though, was that Uxann wasn't sleeping well, couldn't take a doze but to dream discomforting and be threatened awake asweat and awry. In small variations, one particular dream-scene recurred nap time and night sleep. The house was a cave inside a mountain of shade. Light was the food she consumed each morning, and it stole in to her, creeping a winding tunnel, eluding many darkness terrors also hungry for it. And every day, braving the awful challenge, it got through. But visit after visit Uxann noticed it changing, losing brilliance, losing life, except for the eyes. They remained vital, bright as ever—devouring, Gabilan eyes (or the dog-beast's), gleaming yellow like search-beams, and promising betrayal to the darkness.

Awake after whichever version of the dream, if the baby still slept, she'd go from window to window and peek out. If the sun shone, she felt driven to study it, concentrating on the glow of reflections sharp or soft, and the light contrasting to shadows, and the smoky tremulous waves of rising heat, and the glitter and gleam in raindrops, and how the room's slow-floating motes sparkled in shafted sunshine. She washed her mind clean with sunny thoughts, recalling its warmth on her face, the squint it gave to her eye. This way she kept the daydreams, at least, at bay.

But if the baby was awake, it was harder to combat disquiet. For most likely, she'd have to feed, or clean, or comfort him. Which meant watching him close, and facing his strong features, which seemed so wanting to remind her of someone. Which always set her back thinking how, and when, and who.

▼▼▼

WITH HIS ADJUSTED routines, Paps came home early, about threeish. He would hustle through the yard chores, then come inside ready and eager to mind the baby. It might've been mutual, for, in truth, the child seemed at peace in his care, mewling and gurgling contentedly. Confined with it all day, Uxann looked forward to his relief spells, particularly since she got to cook again. Then evening-time was almost like of old, she busying the pots, he tattling village gossip. It was at such times he confided her given status in the village's mind.

"Is lung sickness ah give you. TB. Dat way ah could keep you out of sight without folks wanting to visit. Who want to catch disease in kindness? In fact, some o' dem start shunning me as if I poorly. But ah keep giving dem news, how you coming along, how yuh fall back a little, how ah change medicine, and so on. Off and on, in the rumshop, ah'd be complaining to de fellas how life ent treat me fair at all. Ah'd say, 'Ent Seyeh a decent man?' And everybody will answer, 'Yeah, Seyeh don't deserve he trouble.' Mnn-hmm! Is true dey might be sorry, but remember too, is Seyeh buying. So what else dey can say?"

"So, when I supposed to be getting better?" Uxann asked.

"A while again. A few months," Paps said, his eyes shifting.

"And what about . . ." Uxann indicated the baby snoozing in his arms.

Nodding, teeth aglitter, Paps said lightly. "Watch close, and don't worry. Ah have a plan for dat, too."

Uxann turned back to her pots so he wouldn't notice her face. For no fair reason, his blazing confidence only irritated.

▼▼▼

SHE WAS IN the toilet, on the floor bathing the baby.
The scent of bayleaf and dita payee and gully root—
bush medicines for his skin—rose strong from the basin of warm water. He was gurgling away, enjoying
the water, as she gently massaged each tiny limb with
the soft washcloth. Worries disappeared at times like
this, and handling the miniature perfection of fingers
and toes, her breath caught, he was so marvelous.
Holding his head carefully, she was cleaning the nostrils when, tickled by the cloth's probing tip, the baby
frowned, bunched his forehead into deep furrows, the
already thick, dark eyebrows curved into flapping
wings. It was so exactly the way Paps did, something
clicked in Uxann's mind and trembled her will, and,
hands suddenly weak, she released the infant's head
below the water.

Uxann quickly rescued the coughing, sneezing baby
from distress, then dried and diapered it from fretting,
put on a dusting of talcum and its little sleeping shirt.
Then, heart in her mouth, she held the child to her
shoulder and studied close their reflections in the mir-

ror, already sick-certain she'd recognize Paps again in the baby in her arms. Whatever else the mirror might declare, those eyebrows surely weren't hers!

Done with the viewing, consternation in charge, she carried the baby to her room, and lay with it on her bed to think.

Was it Paps who had breeded her? She quivered with horror at the thought. If so, how? and when? If not him, who else? She could recollect no possibilities. Gradually, though, eliminating event by event in the months past, the night of roughing him in his bed came to mind. That had to be it, she reasoned, and concentrated, trying to recall details. There was no other time she had been even close to a man. But all she remembered was he drunk defenseless, talking about wanting to do Keah, and her ugly response of beating him up, passing out, then boozily returning to her bed. She couldn't even invent more.

Then, thinking harder, more vaguely, she recalled her earlier dizzy about the yard, and dropping bazodie in the cow-pen. Was it then it happened? Had some passing hunter breeded her while in that stupor? Or a jumbie? Or Seyeh come out to pee? Each notion was stupid! And as impossible. Was all senseless, but for the cringy numbness at having been taken advantage of. By anyone. Particularly if it was Seyeh. And she closed in with him these long days.

At that thought, in her soul's keep, a horror cracked its cocoon.

▼▼▼

THEY WERE IN the inside kitchen, Uxann peeling dasheen, Paps nursing the baby fresh-squeezed orange juice from a soaked piece of twine. Uxann's mind was far away, in respite from her troubles for the moment.

"Ah wonder!"

Paps' voice startled her so, the knife slipped through the dasheen peel and sliced a small gash in her thumb. "Huh!" she said, sticking the sharp sting in her mouth.

Paps, engrossed in feeding the baby, hadn't noticed her mishap. Voice innocent–innocent, he said, "Well, ah wonder if yuh have any in mind yet."

Alerted by his tone, Uxann said carefully, "Any what?"

Paps threw her a quick, wry glance. "Well, we can't keep calling him 'Baby,' " he said.

A shock arrowed her guts and riled her as she sensed his bent. This name talk, this christening he'd started bringing up all the time. But how could he be thinking so? Uxann stared at them together, faces peas in a pod, and sucked her bleeding thumb without answering, until Paps flicked her an eye again. Reining her skittish thoughts, she said calmly, "I still thinking."

"Well, is mainly your business, but if yuh seeking, I have a couple ready," Paps returned dryly.

▼▼▼

THESE DAYS SHE was so tired, she was growing a suspicion that the baby was sucking the life out of her as punishment. Not that she lacked milk—her breasts kept flowing like a mountain stream, although she couldn't figure the source, for lately, too, she had no appetite, and was hardly eating. And with her sleeping badly, popping awake alert for she didn't know what, the only thing certain was how she was draining as if something ugly were feeding on her mind. Even her tactic of avoiding thinking child matters was turning out mind pains and hurt. Every day now, a headache would start early and grow as if some jumbie had nothing else to do with buckets and buckets of wicked, hot mud. . . .

▼▼▼

QUITE AFTER DARK and Paps still out—only on payday Fridays since the baby—Uxann, as usual, was exhausted; for hours now the baby had been whiny and whimpering. He wouldn't take her nipples—her usual solution to his any discomfort. And the only trick preventing him from actually crying out loud was the jarring monotony of her walking the floor and jigging him up and down in the cradle of her arm, the briefest pause threatening noise, frazzling her to the edge of exhaustion. A while ago, still with energy for anger, she'd given in to a spell of fierce shaking intentioned more as discipline than easing him. It made no difference. The child's discomfort persisted on the brink of clamour. So again she trekked from one room to another, back, forth, and returning, through countless weary arm changes and tightening shoulders, until even her will began to wear down, and muscles are only flesh. Then, desperate, the open toilet door suggested oasis, a safe place, maybe, to let him loose, and rest. Deepest in the house, in there he was least likely to be heard. So in she went and closed the door, sank down on the toilet cover, and at last! stopped jigging her arms.

She put him in her lap on his back, and let her arms fall slack as relief seeped through her neck and shoulders. She glanced with distaste at the cause squirming in her lap, and caught it shifting eyes and bunching brows exactly like Seyeh pretending surprise. A knot twisted down in her stomach as she thought of Paps' madness for a christening. The child was the mirror of his face. Could anybody see him next to it and not realize him as father? Nobody else was blind.

Right then, as if done ascertaining he was not happy, the child vented a wail to outbray a jackass. No contest, at all. Uxann instantly snatched him up, and returned to her arm-jigging motion—right bounce, right vigour—until Baby once more had control of the peace.

▼▼▼

PAPS EVENTUALLY SHOWED up, jolly but far from drunk. Uxann told him what she needed to. He took the whimpering baby, felt under its neck, put an ear to its belly.

"Dat's an easy one," he said with a snap of his fingers. "De lion will sleep tonight. Is but some wind whining 'e belly, and I have de cure."

He went off and returned with a brown vial. "Dip yuh finger in a drop o' dis paregoric, an' put it on 'e tongue."

Five minutes after, puling done, Baby was asleep.

Exhausted, dozing off, a last wisp of thought: How could it be a good father like Seyeh?

▼▼▼

UXANN WOKE UP sharp-minded, but feeling vaguely disoriented, and had to range around her mind before realizing what it was. She wasn't tired. She had had a full night's sleep. This in mind, she rolled onto her right side to the inside of the bed, where the child slept in a swaddle between the wall and a pillow.

Arms pumping excitedly like rubber gone wild, he lay on his back big-eyeing the action as he pedaled his feet in the air, a crazy-happy baby in the moment's frame.

Uxann eased off the bed, and went smiling to her toilette.

About to brush her teeth, she heard his first whimpers, and abandoned the intention to scamper and ply him arms and nipples. Then, returned to his real world, she went about her business one-armed as she newly had learned how to.

Yesterday Seyeh had offered her a slice of grafted mango that he had brought home. The flesh was pleasantly firm and custard-flavoured, and first time in a long while, Uxann felt a tinge of yearning. He had set aside a few in a cupboard for her. Putting off one for the privacy of this morning's breakfast only fattened the anticipation.

Treat as promised, she was almost done with it before having to change breasts, as the child's impatient pull on her slowing teat came like a tug to a stubborn donkey in her belly. Her nowadays brittleness rushed back and tainted her taste for the mango and, sour-faced, she threw it in the sink. Milk should be bitter, she thought.

Reminded, though, from embers in the ash, she raised a clean flame with some brambles, and put a pot of water over it. Then it was back to nursing, pacing about the rooms, awaiting the child's satisfaction, while running over her plans for when he was done. And running them over, and running them over . . .

The nipple slipped away with a *plop!* and the infant wriggled himself a contented burp. His eyes were closed as if in a doze, but to make sure, Uxann got the medicine bottle and dipped a drop on her little finger. Wasn't hard to persuade him to suck it off, and soon he was fast asleep in his bed-fold. Then Uxann got on with her business.

She chose a shirred school-skirt that had got muddied during a rainy tramp. When the stained patch had persisted despite several washings and sun-bleachings, she'd damned it to the floor of her bottom drawer. It was there, forlorn for forgiveness when she reached, and, spread wide and assessed, it suited.

But first was the paste. She took the bag from the cupboard, and slowly stirred a cup of flour into the slowly bubbling water, taking it off the fire and mixing rapidly as it thickened nicely. There was another ingredient she thought she should add, but couldn't recall from her arts-and-crafts class. Her pot of paste fingered satisfactorily gummy though, and after it cooled to body warmth, she took it to the toilet with the rest of her materials.

She smeared it on with her hands, standing on a chair to reach and well cover every part. Then she spread the skirt all over the paste, pressing it on until the stickiness oozed through to her fingers. When it held by itself, she stepped down and picked up the hammer. Back up on the chair was unwieldy, so it was from the floor she made her first swing, and with a crunch the mirror shattered. But only where she struck it.

Momentarily stunned that it hadn't broken into ten thousand bits and pieces, she had to gather will to de-

liberately hit the squashiness all over. But, not too long
after, it splintered, and a mass of winged darkness
sharded her mind, flapping wildly to maintain awkward
balance, hungry to fly.

The rest was easy. She made a neat bundle of the
wreckage and folded that in a towel, and hid the package up under her bed, next to the wall. She then returned the hammer to its drawer. Next was cleaning the
scant mess in the toilet, which soon was shipshape, and
fit for her sigh for a job well done and a catastrophe
postponed. With no chance now of Seyeh seeing himself
and the child face-to-face, maybe the monster in her
mind would grant some breathing room, and spare her
its fury!

▼▼▼

SEYEH WAS SO one-eyed about the child, he might not
have noticed the mirror. At least, he never mentioned it.
And neither did Uxann. What he kept fishing around
for was a time for naming. They couldn't be a moment
together without him casting lines. In the kitchen one
evening, she cooking, he having the child slurp honey-
comb, his first try: "Ah think he eyes go be he strong

point, he charm. De look in dem come straight from yuh, in truth."

Him talking about whose features! She couldn't help cutting him a glance.

It had been bait and his crooked grin was waiting for her. "Just what ah preaching yuh," he said smugly. "Yuh should see yuh eye. Lancing, ah telling yuh. Lancing like light."

Then, as she returned to her stirring, he added, "Dat'd be a good one. Lance. It have a rightness to it. Yuh don't think?"

She didn't turn around; just clenched her teeth and closed her eyes a moment. Didn't stop the rope from her heart to her guts as it twisted one more knot, though. It just paused the time so that she could draw a small calabash of rainwater and sip a bit before she said her usual "Is a nice name."

THIS TIME HE didn't let it go. She had stewed him a dried–pigeon-pea pelau with fresh pork-skin for meatless grease, and he had downed it with belching relish while she nursed the child in her room. Milk-filled plus a private drop to the tip of his tongue, he was well away to dreamland. With a spoonful of the pelau in a bowl, hesitating, Uxann had joined Seyeh at the lonely table.

"Girl Chile," he said, "is a true-true talent yuh have in yuh hand." He rubbed his belly and heaved a sigh. "Is not for long, but ah hate to have to miss it at all. I saying, with your pots, 'Every day is a milestone.' "

Right away she picked up the design of his tones, and regretted she had tried for his company. But sat in, she played the game. Eye to her bowl, she asked, "Yuh going somewhere?"

"Well, sooner or later, we all have to. Not true?" he said ambiguously.

Same way unclear, Uxann returned, "Well, I hoping to get there late as I can, if I have to."

"No ifs or buts about dis. An' time's afleeting."

Uxann, dreading that he'd pursue the topic, remained silent.

"Is almost three months, Girl Chile," he said. "We gotta name 'im. Is not right an' holy if we don't."

Starting up, Uxann shook her head, protesting automatically, "No . . ."

"No. Yuh wait," Seyeh commanded. "Yuh mustn't be worried about anything. Yuh must realize dat ah have it all work out. All figured down to the smallest item, even caring for the animals, and everything. Yuh have to stay calm and listen to de plan. Is going to be okay. Ah wouldn't betray yuh, we secret. No. No excuse. Stay dere and listen . . .''

Uxann put her bowl on the table and sat back, trapped in the chair.

Seyeh spoke slowly and confidently, in a reasoning manner suggesting the perfection of his ideas. He went on at length with details of personal debts owed him, and about the debtors' stolid reliability. He mentioned a priest in a village a day uphill by donkey, a great friend, this good man was. All benediction, he'd have no questions but the baby's names. He'd do his job and go.

Seyeh had plans for afterwards, too. There was a person who'd hold it for a few months. During this time Uxann would re-establish in the village, maybe even return to school. Then they'd bring back the child, ''adopting'' it from a relative in trouble.

Seyeh was as persuasive as a preacher. Uxann, however, her guts tightening, listened unconvinced. But for the broader outlines, she didn't really hear much of his pitch. Beyond a sensible answer, one query had long commandeered her mind. How would Seyeh explain his same looks with the child?

At the end of it all, he gave her four days. To decide on a name, he said. But not really, as he'd decided to leave this coming Thursday night. All going well, the christening would take place Saturday night.

▼▼▼

WHILE AT HER routines most of the next day, she conceived runaway plans—what clothes to take, what private shortcuts to follow, how far she'd go and leave his child with him. Then, confronted by practicals like destination and money, she abandoned that strategy for futilely fending off despair by blanking her mind.

Burdened with travail, the hours dragged by as slow as boulders growing, and the day passed. And her headaches and the weight of the world gained mass, while her daydreams intermingled with scenes from her past: like dusting down her front-row desk in class; like tramping through the damp woods; like the laughter the day Keah came to work; like a girl in frilly white strolling to church hand in hand with Seyeh.

With darkness, from the bush beyond the backyard, a fearful, monotonous howling filled the hours—the beast-dog lonely? It harried, chasing her from worry to worry, until deep in the night, gathering up child and swaddle, she stole out to answer.

Trying to place the nagging yowls, she prowled

towards the duck pond. From her old spot, she hugged her bundle against the cool darkness, and searched the lair beyond the fence. But, with no feel of its presence, she knew the big beast wasn't there. A whimper in her arms, and, as the mournful howling continued from elsewhere, the loss became linked with the child. And she didn't want to roam the indifferent night anymore. Doleful, she softly returned to her room.

Then came light of another brooding day, then the doldrums of another. Until Seyeh didn't come home with the night.

FRIDAY AWOKE TORPID with a taut feeling of pending hurricane. Trees around the yard stood tall and tense, not a leaf shaking. Through the thin, white, listless curtains, the infant at her nipple, Uxann peeped uneasily at the expectant, grey world. Inside her nostrils felt tight and dry, the tension seeping the air even in the harboured house. All she could hear was the child guzzling at her breast, off and on grunting as he nuzzled it like a piglet. A slight sweat to her skin, from room to room, searching out window to window, Uxann paced patiently and, as he demanded, dutifully changed nipples. Eventually, sated, he released her teat and lay back ready to sleep. Uxann burped him and put him in his swaddle. As he lay comfortably, she made another survey through the windows, then went to the kitchen and took the gripe medicine from the shelf. She checked every window once more before returning to her room. It was about midday, she guessed.

She had to rouse him to get the wet finger in his mouth, but, once there, he promptly sucked it clean. She repeated until his mouth went slack, then wiped his dribble and replaced the medicine half-empty in its spot on the shelf. She let the child be, and returned to patroling the windows. Wasn't long after that the clouds at last burst.

▼▼▼

Rain fell like a reservoir broken. Hour after hour it poured down, clattering on the galvanized roof bucket-a-drop, and hard as bullets. Walking the dim house, Uxann listened, heart atremble, time and again harking—what was that sound?—and rushing to the bedroom door only to see the child soundly sleeping, hissing slightly through his nose. Then back to the window she went, staring at the downpour. Until, drawn back, she stopped agape in the door—the rise and fall of the sleeping bundle stirring her breath again—while the rain pounded down, drumming the galvanize, sounding more and more frantic. But for the sorties past the bedroom, Uxann kept vigil of the murk out the windows. Then, at last, just when outside was getting dark, equal to the violent rattle overhead, she heard the child's frightful wail. And reluctantly relieved, she hastened to duty like a slave.

Hungry, wet, or whatever, he lay kicking and raging his displeasure at the world. Bracing her stomach, Uxann was reaching down for him when, with the rain's roar on the roof balancing out his blaring, she hardly heard his wails, just saw his greedy, twisted face—and surged with rebellion against its terror. "So you want to be bad, well, be bad!" she yelled.

Startled by her volume, the child shut up for a moment. Then, as if surprise re-charged its vim, it returned forcefully to exerting will.

Uxann straightened up with a slow, deep breath. With one look of contempt at the writhing shriek in the swaddle, she turned and left the room, and let it blast away.

With these torrents outside, who was there to hear it? Room to room, she paced and paused to listen. And everywhere, she could hear. Barely sometimes. But she could hear. While time ranted by, the deluge poured down, and the shrieking kept up. While the brooding rage in her mind rustled where it perched, talons pinching viciously as it stretched a hungry neck and pecked spitefully from her tender core. Although her cry was lost to the noise of the flooding world, and the torture in her ears.

Uxann pressed hands to her temples to contain her savaged head. No one's out there, she assured herself, but kept peering through the curtains into the slanting beads of slate-grey rain. There might've been no one. Yet still, she could hear. At whatever window, no matter how far in the house, above the furious weather, above the mauling in her mind, she clearly heard the tyrant's screaming will.

Gradually, the roar of the rain and the rage of his wail flowed into each other like echoes combining stronger, and then thundered into grander echoes again and again re-combined, more and more powerful, until in discrete hollow streams they invaded her head set on emptying each into every resounding chamber they could occupy and forever torment her . . . and quelled by their terrible threat, Uxann surrendered and ran to her purpose.

▼▼▼

Every gulp down his throat was a wrench in her guts. Maybe the exercise to his lungs had given him appetite. But whether it was hunger or something else making him pull so furiously, he was surely pinching of punishment as spice. Twice already Uxann had changed breasts, each time having to battle for possession and control. Relief was past due this present one. She tried slipping it out.

Perhaps it was her tensing, but he anticipated her and increased suction, causing a sharper wince with each pull. She yielded all the breast to him. Yet the wretch wouldn't let up. So she pulled his greedy face into it then—hard, so he'd release her nipple some ease. He was having none of that, and instead sucked in viciously, sending a terrific hot spike up her breast, her whole chest, through her neck burning into her brain, flaring the madly raging midnight wings to swoop and rake and pierce her reason with its awful talons.

She screamed with fury, and squashed the breast into the child's face, to smother-force release. Powered with madness, she rolled over on his little form, adding the full weight of her shoulders to the clamp.

Had to. For he was fighting back, size no measure of his strength, fighting as if equal. Hands and feet and all of little him was squirming, and scratching, and kicking, and writhing, his turtle-beak front gums vise-tight, clenched on the nipple captured in his mouth. A flickering warmth slicked across the pain, and she looked and saw the blood stream over the child's squashed cheeks and swollen eye, then down into the black, curly hair, and over her clamping fingers. A seepage of pale milk joined in, bleeding new horror. *Nooo!* She could stand the agony no more—but she would not submit to the brute. And right on this dagger's point, the struggle seemed to slow, and turn her way, and in awful triumph she screamed again. Anything her mind said. Didn't care. Couldn't hear. Who could with the roars and rages of the rain and the pain commingled?

▼▼▼

HE NEVER LET go his suck on the nipple, and ended with a kick and a shudder that so welled revulsion in her, Uxann couldn't bear its closeness and its pain anymore and, with a hoarse cry, shoved it away. But by the rip of pain she realized the gums were still buried in her tender flesh. Grinning her teeth tight-shut, she screeched a long hum as she prized the jaws apart, squeezing along the cheeks hard with her fingers until the reluctant mouth gaped. Then her teat came free, oozing scarlet and pale; the bottom gum had been halfway into its flesh.

Once free, though, it didn't hurt too badly, except when she rose up from the bed. Palming it support, she went to the kitchen to set a fire going. She was going to need some of that dita-payee/gully-root brew to make a poultice. The water heating, she supported her breast with a rude cloth wrap, and returned to face the matter in her room.

Her every action was careful and deliberate, to manage the business, to regain control, to anchor the confusion whirling her mind. The explanations! What would she tell Seyeh? Say something that wasn't her fault, like an accident in her sleep. Or maybe, a walk in the woods and a fall in the bad weather? Yes, she could say that, or nothing at all, or anything she felt. Or what if she told her nastiest suspicions? How would he take that?

Meantime, she covered its purpled face with a diaper, then wrapped it in strip after strip of the clothes from the swaddle, until it resembled a tight little mummy. Which gave her an idea, and soon she had made a potful of flour paste and daubed it all over the mummy's bandages. Then she wrapped more strips from two old sheets about the pasted mummy, until it was a neat package scented of boiled flour.

On all fours she crawled to the far corner up under her bed, and put the new mummy next to the silent packet of mirror. There it, too, seemed in peace and fitting. Then, keeping busy, she went to attend to her wound, stopping first to indulge in a long drink from the earthen pitcher. Seemed she had been a long time thirsty.

▼▼▼

UXANN SITTING BEHIND the curtains, watching. Out there, a constant background rattle, the riot of rain never quiet. Inside, a battling between a cheek streaked with milk and blood, and the quarrelsome press of futile explanations.

▼▼▼

BELLS. RINGING BELLS. Everywhere bells. Deep, sad ones in black and mourning. Pompous peals dressed Sunday's dawning. A strident one that struck alone. Clatter of the goat-head jumbie going home. *Clang! Clang! Clack! Clack! Blam! Blam! Bap! Bap! Bap!* Another slap! The door! The outside kitchen door!

Uxann leaped from her dream to the fact that she'd slept sitting by the window. It was early light outside. She closed a dry mouth and straightened up, pulling her head from its lean against the wall, where it was more vibrations from the violence at the kitchen door that had aroused her. The dreaded trample of excuses immediately threatening, she rose tensely and tiptoed to the alarm as a bulge of sharp pain reminded of her breast.

The banging began again, accompanied by a clangor of bracelets, and Uxann's heart raced with recognition. At the same time came Keah's voice, impatient and coaxing: "Come on, Uxann. Is me, Keah. Yuh long-time friend. Open the door. Is important, in truth."

Uxann started for the door, then stopped asudden while whats and whys and why-nows mobbed the barricades of her attention.

Keah's voice, urgent and whispering, returned. If she weren't this close, Uxann could not have heard: "Uxann, I know yuh in dere. Ah see yuh sleeping by the living-room window. And I know why yuh waiting. Is for Seyeh, eh?" Voice rising sharply, "Look girl, stop all o' this, and get me out the rain. Ah soaking wet, ah telling yuh.''

It was too much for Uxann to resist. She unlatched the top lock, and swung the top half open. The bright-grey world was still steadily drizzling, but seemed strangely fresh. And with the light, the struggles in her head receded.

Keah pulled back from her sight as if shocked. "Oh, God, girl," she exclaimed, "yuh thin as a ghost! How yuh pale so?''

Older than the few months she hadn't seen her. The lazy, laughing eyes queer and skittish. But basically, the same straight-mouth, stare-down-a-needle Keah, after all. Happy to see her, Uxann busied with the bottom half-door and let her in.

Keah continued her appraisal. "But dat sickness really trim the baby fat off you, girl. Now yu'have figure and waist and everything.''

Unaware of this development till now, Uxann held her surprise quietly, and led Keah to the kitchen, where she flopped into the bentwood chair.

"So how you pad up in one bust like dat?" Keah asked, old molasses voice slow as her assaying eye.

"Ah cut mi'self,'' Uxann said casually.

But then, triggered past first impressions, Keah re-membered the purpose of her visit. She clasped her face with both hands. "Oh, God, Uxann. You wouldn't believe what happen!" Her muffled voice was strained and teary.

Uxann clutched hands to her belly, still halfway missing its solid roundness, and awaited the news.

"What we going to do?" Keah cried.

"What happen?" asked Uxann calmly.

"I can't tell you. How I going to tell you?" sobbed Keah.

Catty-corner in her mind, the neat packages near the wall up under her bed squirmed hazily, and Uxann recalled how Keah was always so passionate and mysterious about stuff. Her troubles never lived up to her drama, though. Cool as dry coconut, Uxann said, "Just tell me what happened."

"De river bridge wash away," Keah choked out. "Dey say it give way foreday morning. . . ."

Uxann watched Keah overreact, anticipating the rest with a twinge of grim relief. Seyeh would be delayed, meaning so could explanations.

Nose snorted clear, Keah continued, "Dey find Joleb's jackass. Find it on the sandbar down by Elbow Basin."

Uxann tried to interpret significance, and failed. To keep Keah talking, she asked, "What they do?"

"Well, what yuh expect dem to do?" exclaimed Keah, dashing bangles in spreading her arms like batie mamzelle. "Bury it? What dey go do with a dead jackass? Cut it open for corbeau?" Then she threw at Uxann pitiful-wet, evasive eyes, and buried her face in her arms on the table to weep.

Uxann felt a sudden qualm that Keah wasn't just carrying on. Something real had happened. Something bad. She went over and gripped Keah's shoulder. "Keah," she said, "what happen? Tell me straight."

Without raising up, Keah sobbed, "How I go tell you dis?"

"You can tell me," Uxann coaxed.

Keah shook her head and wailed, "Noooo."

Uxann squeezed Keah's shoulder firmly. "What happen is really bad?"

Keah sniffled and nodded.

"It concerning you, or it concerning me?"

Keah nodded again.

Uxann's heart quaked, but she had to broach the question. She swallowed spit down a dry throat, and addressed the dreadful suggestion. "Keah, tell me. Something happen to Paps?"

Keah wailed, "Ohhhh! Ohhhh!" shaking her head, refusing to answer.

Uxann could bear it no longer. She grabbed Keah's shoulders two-handed. "Look at me, Keah. Turn around and look at me, and tell me straight!" she shouted.

Rocking her head where it rested, Keah spoke into

her arms. "Dey find de donkey since yesterday evening. And dey still can't find Seyeh."

Knees abruptly weak, Uxann crumpled to the hard floor, jarring her wounded breast against the bent-wood chair's back, though the pain only seemed fitting. "Can't find him? What yuh mean, they can't find him?"

"Is all night he missing now. He must've talked to somebody if he okay. He know everybody dese parts."

There came a loosening sting in her bladder. Uxann thought she'd pee on herself. She pulled up her knees, gentle to the sore breast, and hugged them, and rocked tightly.

Half making sense, Keah blabbered on: ". . . really hope so, 'cause I don't know what we going to do . . . what I go do in my condition . . . is nobody for me now . . . Ma sure to put me out permanent once it start to show . . . is only it belonging to Seyeh dat protect me up to now. . . . Oh, God! What I go do? Uxann . . ." In her chair, she shifted towards Uxann. "Uxann, you going to help me. Right? You going to put me up, please? If Seyeh gone, is bad for you true. But it worse for me. You have everything he leave. He tell me dat. Paper in the land office in town, everything. He tell me all kinda secret, private business, Uxann. Even who is yuh real father. Uxann, if Seyeh gone, we have to be friend. Uxann, you and me could manage together. If he gone we could stay here together. I'd work hard. Ah'd change mih ways, in truth. We would get along . . ."

The words, their meanings, bounced off her understanding violently, exploding pangs in her breast as she squeezed herself too hard, shattering her true heart with their splinters.

With the stroking hand on her hair, Uxann heard Keah say, "Girl, we really in trouble. Not so?"

Uxann looked up at her questioningly.

First time bashful, Keah's eyes fell. Then, fluttering slowly as if pulled off lagley, the lids raised and she met Uxann's direct gaze. "Is true," she said, "I making baby for Seyeh. It three, four months inside."

"You making baby for Paps? For my father?" Uxann repeated, her mind swirling stupidly.

Keah got up and walked to the window and pushed the curtains to one side. Out there was still a slight drizzle, Uxann noted absently, as Keah turned around and answered slowly, "Yes, I baking bread in here for yuh Paps, but dat still don't make him yuh father. Is de born truth. Though he raise you father-loving, he did always know."

Uxann glared at her certain face. "You're lying! Paps would never say dat! Never!"

Eyes hard and steady as glass, Keah shrugged. "How else ah would know? Was a bargain when he put out yuh mother—"

"Why he'd tell you dat? Huh? And what else—?" Uxann cut in.

Keah held eyes with her, then, shifting bangles down her wrists, smiled white as chalk. "Believe what you want. But why I would fool you?"

More to conceal her turmoil, Uxann escaped the sincere, glinting gaze as Keah went on, "But yu'don't have to worry, yu'know. Is only me he tell. And only because we was frenning so serious-serious. In truth, we don't have to argue, Uxann. With Seyeh gone, we on each other side. Everything is between you an' me. Is all we own thing, secret and solid. I telling yuh true."

▼▼▼

UXANN WENT TO the window and pushed the drawn curtains farther aside. The damaged breast slightly touched the sill's protruding edge, and a twinge of pain raised a quiver. She contained the tremor silently, and looked outside. Brightening grey, the place seemed a dripping puddle, quietly draining out. Near the ochro tree, a rooster was jerking a slow worm from its hole. Already, poking-headed pullets were habiting the kitchen door, pecking for their morning's rations. The penned animals would surely need attending. A lot to be done; she'd have to soon tackle it.

Behind her, at the fireside, Keah offered timidly, "Yuh want something to eat?"

Without looking around, Uxann said, "Nah. Do for yourself. I have a grafted mango." She remained facing the natural order out there.

No shudders, no show, no tears streamed.

GLOSSARY

bachac	parasol ants
balata	yellow-shelled, sweet, creamy-pulped fruit
batie mamzelle	dragonfly
bazodie	in a stupor or fit
bhagii	variety of spinach
bodie beans	foot-long green beans
breadfruit	edible fruit transplanted by Captain Cook from the South Pacific islands
buffo-buffo	reminiscent of common toad; *Bufo marinus*
buljohl	dish of soaked or boiled codfish with on-ions, etc.
bull-pistle	whip made from stretched and cured bull's penis
caiso	calypso, old-timers' pronunciation
calabash	gourdlike fruit
cassava	manioc
chenette	thick-shelled, sweet-sour, marble-sized fruit
cocoyea	coconut-leaf spines
corbeau	vulture; scavenger raptor
corrily	knobby, bitter-skinned cucumber variety; skin is edible
coscarob	freshwater fish of cychlid species
crapaud	common garden toad; *Bufo marinus*
cymite	star apple

dasheen	ground provision, like eddoes (*yautia* in Spanish)
dita payee	medicinal herb
flambeau	torch made from kerosene in a bottle with a cloth wick
frenning	having a romantic relationship
Gabilan	of raptor species; as large as a peregrine falcon
guanabana	soursop
gully root	medicinal herb
hog-plum	large trees of abundant fruit; used as hog feed
immortelle	red-flowering shade tree common in cocoa plantations
jiggers	hookworm larvae
jumbie	spirit, ghost
kaya	cannabis species
lagley	gum from bled breadfruit-tree trunk, like rubber
leghorn	variety of poultry
liana	tropical forest vine
macawoeul	boa constrictor
maccoe	busybody, nosey parker
manicou	opossum
mauvais-langue	"bad tongue," from French; to bad-mouth
millionfish	guppies
mingy	meager, or mean combined with stingy
morah	a preferred building wood, like mahogany
'Nancy	Anancy, spider trickster of Caribbean folklore
pappyshow	distortion of puppet show
paregoric	morphine-based grippe medicine
pelau	dish of rice, pigeon-peas, and meat stewed together

petite careem	Indian summer
pigeon-peas	common tropical garden-grown legume
pomme cytere	golden apple
pomme-rac	red-skinned, white-fleshed, sour-sweet tropical pear
posie	potty, bedpan
puling	whining, like pewling
sapodilla	brown, rough-skinned, sweet-fleshed tropical fruit
schupid	stupid (country-style pronunciation)
scrungy	similar to *grungy*
sometimishness	undependability, capriciousness
tapia	mud and grass kneaded together to make walls
tattoo	armadillo; wasps with similar-looking hard black shell
vaps	a yen, a whim, a sudden urge
zaboca	avocado
zangee	freshwater lamprey
zebu	hump-necked bovine

ABOUT THE AUTHOR

KELVIN CHRISTOPHER JAMES was born in Trinidad. He holds a B.S. from the University of the West Indies and a doctorate in science education from Columbia University. His short stories have appeared in *Between C & D, BOMB, American Letters and Commentary, Quarto, The Portable Lower East Side, The Literary Review*, and *Les Jungles d'Amerique* in France. In 1989 he won a New York Foundation for the Arts fellowship in fiction. *Jumping Ship and Other Stories* was published in 1992. *Secrets* is his first novel. He lives in Harlem, New York.